Blackbeard's Treasure

by

Kathleen Thomas

Tudor Publishers
Greensboro

First Edition

This is a work of fiction. Other than historical figures, all persons and events depicted in this work bear no resemblance to real persons living or dead, or to actual events.

Library of Congress Cataloging-in-Publication Data

Thomas, Kathleen—1943

Blackbeard's Treasure / by Kathleen Thomas—1st ed.

p. cm.

Summary: While attending summer camp on Cape Hatteras, North Carolina, four cousins, aged eight to fourteen, become involved in the search for the pirate Blackbeard's lost treasure ship, the "Queen Anne's Revenge."

ISBN 0-936389-99-0 (alk. paper)

(1. Pirates—Fiction. 2. Salvage—Fiction. 3. Buried Treasure—Fiction. 4. Blackbeard, d. 1718—Fiction. 5. Queen Anne's Revenge (Sailing vessel)—Fiction. 6. Camps—Fiction. 7. Brothers and Sister—Fiction. 8. Cousins—Fiction. 9. Outer Banks (N.C.)—Fiction. I. Title

PZ7.T36698Blb 2008

(Fic)—dc22

2008027378

For Diane and Herman

Contents

Chapter 1: The Adventure Begins 7

Chapter 2: A Tale by Firelight 14

Chapter 3: The Old Sailor 20

Chapter 4: Boats and Dreamboats 32

Chapter 5: Attack at Sea 38

Chapter 6: A Mysterious Intruder 46

Chapter 7: The Ghost Appears 51

Chapter 8: Humiliation 55

Chapter 9: Danger in the Depths 60

Chapter 10: Storm 68

Chapter 11: Treasure at Last... 81

Chapter 12: Catching the Crooks.................................. 88

Chapter 13: The Real Treasure.................................... 102

Bibliography 105

Chapter 1

The Adventure Begins

"The Outer Banks!" shouted ten-year-old Lauren Prakke, her eyes shining. "We can go swimming and sand surfing and see 'The Lost Colony.' "

"And pirates!" chimed in her older brother, thirteen-year-old Matthew. "You guys gotta come with us."

This comment was directed at their cousins, Haley and Luke Prakke, aged twelve and nine, respectively. Matthew and Lauren lived in Raleigh, North Carolina, while Haley and Luke lived in nearby Cary. Their fathers were brothers and the children had been lifelong playmates.

"Sure!" shouted Luke, jumping up from his chair on his cousins' patio. "What do we have to do?"

"Both of us are going to Y camp this summer, and we can each invite a guest," explained Lauren. "It will be loads of fun."

"We'll have to ask Mom and Dad," replied Haley, but I bet they'll say yes."

"Great!" shouted Matthew raising both fists in the air. "We were wondering what to do with you guys this summer. What an adventure!"

A month later, a bus full of twenty-five boisterous, vivacious children left Raleigh, but after five hours they were all pretty worn out and bored with the monotonous scenery rolling past. Some were listening to ipods, others were playing video games, others sleeping.

Lauren looked over at her brother, who was deep in a book. "Whatcha reading?" she asked, only half-interested.

"It's a book about a pirate," he muttered without looking up.

"Which one?"

"Blackbeard. He sailed around the Outer Banks about 1712," Matthew responded, glancing up at his sister, skeptical that a girl could appreciate anything as fascinating as pirates. "He was killed off the coast of Ocracoke."

Lauren yawned and said nothing. Matthew smirked, his suspicions confirmed.

But Luke was another story. "Blackbeard!" he exclaimed. "I've heard of him. Let me see."

Matthew surrendered the book to his cousin, aware that he was sharing a sacred object with a fellow true believer.

"Wow! Look at that," shouted Luke. He pointed to a picture of the notorious pirate, depicting a huge man in a black tricorner hat, brandishing a cutlass and a pistol. A flowing black beard wreathed his fierce countenance, rendered more frightening by slow-burning rope matches placed under the rim of his hat. "Read it out loud," pleaded Luke.

Matthew smiled and retrieved the book. " 'Blackbeard, whose real name may have been Edward Teach, plied the waters of the Caribbean and the South Atlantic coast from 1710 to 1712,' " he read.

"Plied?" asked Luke.

"Yeah. You know, sailed."

"Oh."

" 'He captured ships from Barbados to the Outer Banks of North Carolina before his ship, the *Adventure*, was trapped in Ocracoke Inlet and he was killed by Lt. Robert Maynard of the Royal Navy on November 22, 1712,' " read Matthew. " 'His most infamous act was anchoring outside Charleston harbor to stop all ships going into or coming out of the busy port to exact tribute from the city's merchants.' "

"Infamous?" queried Luke.

"Wicked," replied an exasperated Matthew. "How am I ever going to finish if you keep interrupting?"

"Sorry," answered a chastened Luke. "Does it say anything about making women walk the plank?"

"Uhm, let's see," muttered Matthew, scanning the page. "No, but listen to this:

" 'During his career, Blackbeard is said to have seized twenty-three ships and gold and jewels worth a fortune. Although he squandered huge sums in riotous living in various ports in the West Indies, rumors persist that he buried much of it on isolated islands along the Outer Banks and the Caribbean, which has never been recovered.' "

"Buried treasure!" exclaimed Luke. "I knew it!"

"And they never found it," Lauren said in a bored, singsong tone as she rolled her eyes. Haley giggled.

"Girls," Matthew pronounced dismissively. "Pay no attention to them. I bet if we used this book as a guide we could find that treasure."

"Like nobody's been looking for it for the last three hundred years," sneered Lauren.

Before the boys could answer, the voice of Dave Phillips, camp counselor, boomed over the bus intercom.

"Okay, boys and girls, listen up. We will be arriving at Camp Ocracoke in a few minutes. I want you to gather up all your things and be ready to get off as soon as the bus stops. After you line up I want the trip captains to distribute the bags to each camper. Let's all cooperate, because we have a lot to do today. Okay?"

A loud chorus of "okays" replied, then the bus exploded in a flurry of boys and girls throwing cards, video games, and books into backpacks. Screams of protest greeted those who stood on the arms and legs of their companions to pull luggage down from the overhead racks. Dave smiled, shook his head and turned around to speak to the bus driver.

Ten minutes later the bus pulled into a large parking lot, where a small group of camp counselors were waiting to greet the bus.

"Everybody off the bus and line up," said Dave. "Karen

Scott will hand out your registration forms and cabin assignments. Please try to keep it down to a mild roar."

He might as well have saved his breath, as the horde of youngsters scrambled down the bus aisle and squeezed out the door.

"Hey, quit shoving!," hollered Luke as he was pushed through the door. "You're mashin' me!"

Somehow, Dave and Karen got the kids lined up and the appropriate forms distributed. Matthew grabbed Luke's arm. "The guys are in cabin number four. Girls are in cabin five," he said.

"We know perfectly well which cabin we're in," said Haley, haughtily. "We don't need any boys to tell us what to do." She and Lauren turned and walked through the door of their cabin, a one-story log structure with a screened porch running the entire length of the front side.

Matthew and Luke entered their own cabin. There were two rows of bunk beds with a rolled-up mattress and a pillow at the foot of each bunk. A single, unshaded light bulb dangled over every fourth bunk.

"We've got bunks twelve and thirteen," said Matthew, looking at the slip of paper in his hand.

"I'll take bunk twelve," said Luke. "I don't want any part of number thirteen."

"What's the matter, are you superstitious or something?" laughed Matthew. "Come on."

Their footsteps echoed on the pine floor. They squinted as they tried to read the numbers painted in white on the end rails of the bunks. There were only two windows, one on each side of the cabin, and the door at the end, Staring into the semi-darkness, they located their bunks—the last two on the left.

"Hi," said a voice behind them. They turned to see a tall, thin boy with dark hair and horn-rimmed glasses standing by the next bunk. "I'm Harold Allen. I was here last year, so I can show you the ropes. Everybody just stows their stuff under the bunks."

"""We're Matthew and Luke Prakke," replied Matthew.

"Praykee?"

"It's pronounced Prah-*ka*," said Matthew.

"What kinda name's that?" asked Harold. "Sounds weird."

"It's Dutch," answered Luke defensively. But Harold's smile was so friendly that neither boy took offense.

"Are you brothers?"

"No, cousins," said Matthew. "We each have a sister over in the girls' cabin."

"You brought your *sisters*?" asked Harold incredulously.

"We didn't have any choice," said Matthew. "But it's okay. They're cool . . . for sisters."

"Well, anyway, they'll be calling everybody over to the dining hall for dinner any minute now. Are you hungry?"

"I'll say!" shouted Luke, throwing his backpack under his bunk. "What are we having?"

"Mystery meat, probably," shot back Harold. "But don't worry, the snack bar has some pretty good stuff. Just be sure to bring lots of change."

"So where are you from?" said a tall, redheaded girl, who towered over Lauren and Haley.

"Raleigh," replied Lauren. "And you?"

"Joanna Livingston, one of *the* Livingstons of Charlotte." She announced it as if she expected expressions of awe from the other two. When they just smiled and said nothing, her stare became icy and her manner aloof. "I'll be your cabin leader. There aren't many rules, so that shouldn't be a problem. First of all, what are your names?"

I'm Haley Prakke, and this is my cousin, Lauren Prakke."

"What kind of . . . "

"It's Dutch," said Haley, cutting off the question she had come to expect over the years.

"Whatever. The bathrooms are over there," she said, pointing toward the other end of the room, "but the showers are in the building outside. As soon as you get your things put away, come to the meeting by my bunk. We're going to have elections for my assistants. Hurry up."

With that, Joanna abruptly turned and walked away.

"Wow, Miss Personality," said Lauren. She watched as Joanna whispered to another girl, then began laughing. She could just imagine what catty things those girls were saying about the two of them.

"Well, we're *the* Prakke girls from Raleigh," said Haley, giving her cousin a punch on the arm. "Come on, let's get squared away and then enter the lion's den."

"Meow," laughed Lauren.

"Okay," said Joanna in a loud voice, addressing the circle of ten girls seated in folding chairs in the commons area just inside the front screen door. "This is how it works. "I have been designated the cabin leader because I was an assistant last year. You get to elect two girls to act as my assistants. The rules are posted on a sheet of paper beside the door, but they are pretty simple. One, everyone up at seven; two, breakfast at the dining hall at seven-thirty; three, lights out at ten o'clock; and four, do what I say."

A ripple of laughter started at this last rule, but quickly died out as everyone saw from Joanna's expression that she wasn't kidding.

"Let's get started," snapped Joanna. "Raise your hands if you want to nominate someone for cabin assistant." A flurry of hands shot up, but from the way Joanna carefully chose the applicants, it was evident that she had pre-selected whom she would recognize.

"I nominate Sally Jessup," said one girl.

"And I nominate Carol Baker," said another.

"What's your name?"

Lauren turned to see a short, blonde-haired girl with blue eyes smiling at her.

"Lauren Prakke." Lauren waited for the inevitable question, but when it didn't come, she smiled back.

"I nominate Lauren Prakke," said the girl. She even pronounced it correctly, which was no small shock to Lauren.

After several more names were placed in nomination, Joanna declared the election closed and slips of paper and pencils were passed around. In a few minutes Joanna collected them, then announced the results.

"Sally Jessup and Carol Baker have been selected as my assistants. Now let's all go over to the dining hall for dinner."

The chairs were pushed against the wall and the girls filed out of the cabin, either in small groups or individually.

"I could have told you they would be 'elected,' " said the girl who had nominated Lauren. "I saw Joanna talking to them when I came into the cabin. The whole thing was rigged."

"Then why did you nominate Lauren?" asked Haley.

"I liked the way she wasn't impressed with our 'Fearless Leader' when she introduced herself to you. I got here early, and right away I sized her up as more of a prison matron than a 'cabin leader.' I'm Lucy Parker."

"Lucy, I think we're going to be friends," said Lauren, shaking hands and introducing Haley.

"Me too," answered Lucy. "Now let's get some chow. I'm starved."

Chapter 2

A Tale by Firelight

"I'm stuffed," sighed Luke. He plopped down on a log outside the girls' cabin.

"You should be. I never saw anyone put away so many hot dogs," mumbled Haley, stretched out on the ground, too weary to acknowledge the presence of Lauren and Matthew as they came up and took seats beside Luke.

They had spent the day wandering around, becoming familiar with the layout of the camp and randomly meeting the other campers. The camp was laid out in the middle of a pine barren, with four cabins, a dining hall and a recreation hall surrounding a square dominated by flagpoles, from which flew the United States and North Carolina flags. A trail led off among the dunes to the beach. Supper had been hot dogs and beans served at picnic tables outside the dining hall.

"Don't get too comfortable," warned Matthew. "I heard Dave say there is going to be a big bonfire down on the beach, where he's going to tell stories. Like now."

The other three groaned and struggled to their feet. They saw Karen waving everyone down the trail to the beach. Despite their fatigue—and Luke's bloated condition—they were intrigued as they emerged from the woods and out onto the beach. The waves crashed loudly and the wind whipped with surprising intensity as they joined a circle of kids surrounding a huge, crackling fire. Sparks shot up in a dazzling whirlwind, only to be lost in the night sky. A circle of boys and girls surrounded the fire, listening intensely as

Dave talked to several kids.

As soon as the campers were all seated around the fire, Dave said, "It's a tradition here at Camp Ocracoke to tell stories around the campfire on the first night. "So what shall it be?" He looked around the group, waiting for suggestions.

"Tell us some pirate stories!" Luke piped up. A chorus of cheers greeted his idea.

"Okay," agreed Dave. "Who do you want to hear about?"

"Stede Bonnet," one camper shouted.

"Captain Kidd," screamed out another.

"How about women pirates," said Haley.

"That's silly," snorted Luke. "Everybody knows there weren't any female pirates."

"Oh, but there were," countered Dave. "Anne Bonney and Mary Wall were two of the most notorious pirates that ever lived."

Haley turned to smile smugly at Luke.

"Blackbeard!" shouted Matthew.

"All right," said Dave, "that seems only right, seeing as how he was the most famous pirate to sail these waters. To begin with, nobody knows exactly what his real name was, or where and when he was born. But most folks believe his name was Edward Teach, and he was born in Bristol, England, in 1688. He joined the Royal Navy as a lad of sixteen to fight in Queen Anne's War against Spain. Some say that is why he named his most famous ship the *Queen Anne's Revenge*." He pointed out beyond the crashing waves to the vast, dark ocean. "During his career of piracy he plied these waters for years, capturing ships loaded with treasure." All eyes turned toward the ocean, but none were as enraptured as those of Matthew and Luke. "He commanded a small fleet of three ships and over one hundred men."

"And he took twenty-three ships and treasure worth millions!" shouted Luke, impatient for Dave to get on with the story.

"Well, it looks like we have some real pirate historians with us," said Dave. Luke and Matthew blushed and ducked their heads as hoots erupted from the other campers.

"That's right, he is supposed to have taken twenty-three ships," continued Dave. "But his loot was more like thousands of dollars, not millions. He became such a menace to merchants' ships along the Atlantic seacoast that Governor Spottswood of Virginia eventually commissioned Lt. Robert Maynard to hunt him down. He searched for weeks before finally finding Blackbeard's ship, the *Adventure*, in Ocracoke Inlet, out there." He pointed off to his right. But Blackbeard was a clever man, and tricked Maynard into running his ship aground on a sandbar." Dave's voice sank to a hoarse whisper. "Now Blackbeard closes in for the kill. He orders his gunners to fire a broadside, which sweeps the deck of Maynard's ship, killing a number of his sailors."

Just at this moment, the fire popped loudly, sending up another round of sparks into the dark sky. Everyone jumped and squealed in fright.

Dave smiled and continued. "Men lie in pools of blood and shriek in agony as Blackbeard orders another broadside. When the smoke clears, Maynard and his first mate are the only ones left standing. 'Throw the grappling hooks' shouts Blackbeard, drawing his huge saber. 'And board her, Mateys. No prisoners!' When the ships are side by side, Blackbeard is the first aboard, followed his crew."

"And they killed Lt. Maynard and sank his ship, didn't they?" shouted out Matthew breathlessly.

"*No!*" Dave shouted back. "Lt. Maynard has a trick of his own. Just as the pirates spread out over the deck, dozens of Royal Navy sailors and mariners come out of the hatches and attack the unsuspecting pirates. You see, they are hiding below decks to make the pirates think the crew is all dead. The pirates are so surprised that those who aren't killed or captured, jump into the ocean and try to return to their own ship."

"What happened to Blackbeard?" asked Harold, who by now was as caught up in the story as Matthew and Luke.

"Well, Blackbeard is no coward," continued Dave. "He fights ferociously, drawing and firing all of the pistols that he carries in a belt across his chest. Then he draws his cutlass, and spying Lt. Maynard, roars out a challenge. 'Now I'll send ye to the infernal regions!' He strikes such a fierce blow that it breaks Maynard's sword in two. With a fiendish laugh, he raises his cutlass to deliver a death blow."

"Then what?" said Luke in a hushed voice.

"Just as Blackbeard is about to kill Maynard, a British sailor strikes Blackbeard a savage cut on his neck. The huge pirate staggers and collapses to the deck, struggling to rise up again, then falls back, dead."

A deathly silence descended over the listeners, as they waited for the end of the story.

"Maynard cuts off Blackbeard's head and hangs it from the prow of his ship. Then he has Blackbeard's body thrown overboard."

Several girls wrinkled up their noses and said, "Ugh, that's disgusting."

"Then the most incredible thing happens," added Dave. "Before it sinks, they say that Blackbeard's body swam three times around Maynard's ship!"

A series of gasps erupted from the audience. Matthew glanced over at Lauren and Haley, who were tightly clutching each other's hands. When Lauren saw him smiling at them, she quickly dropped Haley's hand, and nodded toward Luke. Matthew turned to see him staring transfixed at Dave, his mouth open.

"Maynard returns to Bath and receives a reward for killing Blackbeard and capturing his crew. Once Blackbeard is gone, the 'Age of Piracy' in the Caribbean comes to an end."

"What happened to Blackbeard's head?" Luke shouted, at last snapping out of his trance.

Dave smiled wickedly, as if he had been waiting for that question. "No one knows for sure. Some say Maynard kept it as a trophy, others that Governor Spottswood took it to show distinguished guests from England. After a few years it supposedly disappeared, no one knows where. But one rumor has it that Blackbeard's ghost came back for it, so that he could put it back on his shoulders in order to look for the treasure he buried here on the Outer Banks."

Silence greeted the end of the story; no one dared speak. Dave looked around, obviously pleased with his storytelling talent. They had wanted a good ghost story by firelight, and he had given it to them. "Well, I guess that about does it for tonight. Shall we get these kids to bed, Karen? It's going to be a busy day tomorrow."

Slowly the campers rose and followed Karen along the trail through the sand dunes back to the cabins. Very few campers walked alone, most of them clustered in groups, nervously peering into the dark around them.

"Can we walk with you?" said Lauren, holding Haley's hand.

"What's the matter," sneered Luke. "Did Dave's story scare you?"

"Didn't it scare you?" shot back Haley.

"Naw," scoffed Luke. "Everybody knows there's no such thing as ghosts."

"Yeah," chimed in Matthew. "No way a headless body is gonna swim three times around a ship."

"Let's don't talk about it," Lauren said quickly, waving her hands. "Just walk with us, and keep your mouth shut about it." She shot both of the boys a warning look that threatened dire consequences if they told anyone how frightened she and Haley were.

"Okay, come on," said Matthew, putting Lauren on his left side, and Haley on his right, and throwing his arms protectively around their shoulders. When Luke attempted to do the same with Haley, she impatiently pushed him away—but not too far.

The boys said good night to their sisters at the door of the girls' cabin, then walked on to their own. Exhausted, Matthew crawled under the covers.

"Weren't those girls silly to be so scared over a dumb old ghost story?" said Luke, his voice muffled by the covers.

"Yeah, I guess," replied Matthew. "But you have to admit it was a good one." Luke didn't answer, and just as Matthew was about to drift off to sleep, he heard a click. He turned to see a faint light shining under Luke's sheet. It puzzled him at first, until he realized it was a flashlight.

Matthew grinned. "Some pirate you'd make," he mumbled as he turned back and buried his face into his pillow.

Chapter 3

The Old Sailor

The next morning was filled with learning the routines of camp, what the counselors called "housekeeping chores." Reveille at 7:00. Clean cabin from 7:00 to 7:30. Breakfast at 8:00. Announcements and camp chore assignments at 8:30. Crafts and woodlore from 9:00 to 12:00 noon. By 1:00 everyone was looking forward to "free time," where they could choose what *they* wanted to do in the afternoon, until dinner at 5:00, when they were once again squeezed into what the grown ups thought they wanted to do.

Luke sauntered up to where Matthew, Lauren, and Haley were studying the long list of "free time" activities posted on the bulletin board outside the dining hall.

"Wow," he sighed, "who'd have thought summer camp was just another name for prison."

"Oh, come on," his sister said, rolling her eyes, "it isn't that bad. But I'm tired of all this 'directed activity.' "

"Yeah, it's like they're afraid if we do our own thing, our minds will turn into guava jelly," scoffed Matthew.

"Well, there's a whole lot of things listed here that we can do," said Lauren. "How about swimming at the lake?"

"Nah," said Haley, wrinkling up her nose. "We'll get to do that every day. Isn't there something different we can do?"

"Okay," replied Lauren, "softball, badminton, horseshoes, tennis . . . "

Each activity was greeted with deafening silence.

"I said *different*," protested Haley. "An adventure."

"Here's something that sounds interesting," said Matthew. "A sightseeing trip into Ocracoke."

"Now you're talking!" perked up Haley. "We can go shopping."

"Girl stuff!" said Luke.

Matthew frowned. "I was thinking more like the lighthouse, the Maritime Museum . . . "

"Boy stuff!" Haley and Lauren moaned in unison.

"Well, we can take the bus and split up when we get to town," reasoned Haley. "You guys can go your way, and we'll go ours."

"Done!" shouted Luke.

"You want to invite Harold?" asked Matthew, turning to Luke. "He seemed like an all right kinda guy." Luke nodded.

"And there's a girl in our cabin that would like to go with us."

Without further ado, Matthew signed the bus trip schedule and by 1:30 they were all aboard the bus. Except for Karen as chaperone, the Prakkes and their friends were the only passengers.

"So much for 'adventure,' observed Lauren.

"Aw, you guys will have fun, trust me," said Lucy.

"I remember climbing up to the top of the lighthouse last year," said Harold "You can see for miles and miles."

"I'm signing up for softball, first thing when I get back," muttered Luke. "And horseshoes, badminton . . ."

In twenty minutes they were standing on a street corner in Ocracoke. Karen had told them to meet her at the base of the lighthouse for the tour at 3:30.

"You can see from one end of the 'town' to the other without moving," complained Luke.

"The shops are over there," said Lucy, pointing across the street. "We girls will go there. Harold can show you where the sports shop is. And the museum is one street over, with all that geeky naval stuff. You guys enjoy."

Leaving the girls to the unimaginable 'pleasures of shop-
'

ping, the guys walked slowly into the museum. Expecting to see only boring exhibits of seafaring equipment, they were ecstatic to see ship models and paintings and pictures of rescues and sea battles, from the seventeenth century up to World War II.

But it wasn't until Luke walked into a large room that he stood transfixed and open-mouthed. When Matthew and Harold asked him what was wrong, all Luke could do was point silently at a sign hanging from the ceiling, which read: "Blackbeard Exhibit."

As if in a daze, Luke approached a large glass case housing a model of the *Queen Anne's Revenge*. With difficulty, Harold dragged him over to cases of pirate weapons and clothing. And when the Prakke boys came upon a full-length painting of the pirate in all his regalia, they almost sank to their knees.

"That's not all," said Harold, pointing to another wall. "Look at that." Before them hung a painting of the infamous pirate's last battle. There he was, at the point of cleaving Lt. Maynard in two with his massive sword.

An hour later, they reluctantly left the museum. "Why didn't anybody tell me this place existed?" said Luke. "They should've made the whole place a museum to Blackbeard."

They were startled by raucous laughter behind them. "That's nothin' son. Lookee over there."

Turning around they saw an old man with a white beard smiling at them from a tanned, wrinkled face. He wore a battered sailor's cap that looked as if it had once been white, a blue and white striped tee shirt, and faded jeans. He was pointing at a wooden building painted red, with a white railing bordering a ramp that zigzagged to the front door. A sign identified it as "Teach's Hole."

"That's the best store for gettin' stuff on Blackbeard, if that's what ye want," growled the old salt.

The boys ran across the street and entered the shop. Before them was a wonderland of pirate "stuff": tee shirts, maps of the Outer Banks showing sites of "buried treasure," reproductions of cutlasses and pistols and every imaginable depiction of Blackbeard himself. Lauren, Haley and Lucy were looking through a pile of tee shirts.

"Hey, are you guys getting a shirt?" asked Lauren.

"Nah," scoffed Luke. "I'm getting that pirate flag on the wall."

Sometime later, the girls walked out, followed by the boys weighed down with bags of "loot."

"I thought you guys said shopping was boring," teased Haley. The girls walked over to an ice cream stand.

"All they bought was clothes," said Luke. "But I bought every book on Blackbeard; now I'll know *everything* about him!"

"If you want to learn about Blackbeard, you'll have to go up to Bath and that area." It was the old sailor, fixing them with a steely gaze.

"Huh?" said Luke. "I thought he was all over the Outer Banks."

"And wasn't he killed right over on Ocracoke Inlet," countered Matthew.

"Well, now, the rascal's last battle was fought there, that's a fact," admitted the sailor, squinting out over the water and shading his eyes with his hand.

"Our camp counselor said that when Blackbeard was captured, that was the end of the Age of Piracy," said Luke, defiantly.

"Posh, lad," scoffed the old sailor. "You talk as if he was the only pirate that sailed these waters. Why, there were lots o' pirates in these parts." Seeing the skeptical look on the boys' faces, and sensing he was in danger of losing his audience, he quickly added: "But I reckon he was the worst, no doubt about that!"

"How do know about Blackbeard and the other pirates?" asked Luke.

"Why, I was born and raised right here on the Banks. Been livin' here all my life. My daddy raised me on stories about pirates. And lots o' other tales too. Jim Hawkins is my name. The best sailor there ever was on the Outer Banks."

"He was the boy in *Treasure Island*," said Matthew.

"Aye, that he was, boy," replied Hawkins, his eyes twinkling. "I see we have a reader here. Maybe that's who my daddy named me for. He was always partial to stories of adventure on the sea. And there was a pirate in that tale too, wasn't there? Let's see, his name was . . . "

"Long John Silver," answered Harold.

"But let's get back to Blackbeard," interrupted Luke impatiently.

"Right ye are," said Hawkins, pointing a finger at him. "Why waste time on fake pirates when we can talk about the most famous real pirate there ever was."

"What was that about Bath?" asked Matthew. "I thought he came from Ocracoke."

"No, lad," said Hawkins. "That's just where he was killed. He had a house in Bath. Lived for years there, amongst the gentry, and guests of the richest folks in town. And proud they was to call him their friend, too."

"Can we go there?" asked Matthew.

"Don't see why not," replied Hawkins. "And there's nobody better to take ye there." He jerked a thumb at a sign over his right shoulder. It read: "Outer Banks Tours. Fishing charters and sightseeing. Jim Hawkins, proprietor."

"Do you think the camp will let us go?" asked Luke.

"A group of us went there last year," volunteered Harold. "We had a great time."

"So you're with the summer camp, are ye?" asked Hawkins. "Well, yes, I've taken a group up there from time to time. Just have one o' the counselors give me a call, and we can work somethin' out." He turned to wink at Luke. "I'll make sure it's my special pirate tour."

Luke's eyes were shining, as if he were looking at one of his heroes.

"Say, it's after three o'clock," said Matthew, looking at his watch. "We'd better pick up the girls and go over to the lighthouse."

"Right. Off you go, boys," said Hawkins, waving.

"Where have you *been*?" asked an exasperated Haley. "We've been waiting at this stand forever."

"We met a really cool old sailor who told us all about Blackbeard," said Matthew.

"Blackbeard again," groaned Haley.

"Yeah, and he gives tours, charters boats and stuff," added Luke. "Look, he gave us his card."

"What for?" asked

"So we can ask the counselors to go on a tour of Bath, of course," said Luke.

Both girls rolled their eyes and sighed. "Well, we're supposed to meet Karen and Lucy to go to the lighthouse," said Haley sternly, "and if we don't hurry, we're all going to be in big trouble."

They ran down the street to where the bus was parked and scrambled on board, where Karen was impatiently waiting. In a short time they saw the squat lighthouse looming above them.

"Okay," said Karen, as the bus came to a stop. "We'll all meet at the top. Climb the stairs slowly and stay together. Miss Harris is the park ranger who is going to show us the sights. I want you to be quiet and listen to her respectfully. I also expect you to ask a lot of questions."

As the kids clambered off the bus, Luke and Matthew raced ahead. "Race ya to the top!" shouted Luke as they ran past Haley and Lauren.

"Karen said to climb slowly," yelled Lauren, shaking her head. She might as well have been trying to stop the tide from coming in.

The wind was surprisingly strong at the top, and even Luke was quiet as he looked down at the ground below.

"Oh, isn't it just beautiful?" said Lauren. "You can see forever."

"It *would* be beautiful if I could see," replied Haley, pushing the hair from out of her face for the millionth time.

"I can tell you're Luke's sister," teased Lauren. "There's got to be something wrong with *everything*!"

They looked out at an ocean that melted into the haze.

"And over there is Ocracoke Inlet," said Lucy.

"Ocracoke Inlet! "said Luke. "That's where Blackbeard

was captured! Lemme see." He pushed his way forward, only to be disappointed, as it was obscured by haze and looked just like all of the other inlets Miss Harris pointed out.

"Could you stop thinking and talking about Blackbeard for at least five minutes?" pleaded Lauren. "There's more to the Outer Banks than pirates, you know."

"Not for me," grumbled Luke.

Luke descended the stairs slowly, letting the others rush past him. When he got to the bottom, Matthew looked at him for a moment, then slapped him on the shoulder.

"Come on, snap out of it," he said. "Say, why don't we give Karen Sailor Hawkins' card and ask him if she'll arrange a day trip to Bath and Ocracoke Inlet?"

"Yeah, that would be great!" said Luke.

The boys ran over to where Karen was standing, gave her the card and told him how much they wanted to go on Sailor Hawkins' pirate tour.

"Oh, yes, Mr. Hawkins," she said, smiling. "He's quite a character. He took a group of us on his tour last year. I tell you what, if enough of the others want to go, we'll arrange the trip."

"Hooray!" shouted both boys together.

All the next day Matthew and Luke lobbied the rest of the campers to sign up for the tour of Bath and Ocracoke. Luke was surprised that most of them weren't as excited as he was. One wit even came up with the slogan, "Well, Luke sure could *use* a bath!" It caught on quickly and he had to endure it over and over for the next two days, but he thought it was worth it if enough kids would agree to go. Luke and Matthew used all of their considerable sales talents to work up a crowd

On Thursday the campers lined up for the bus at seven o'clock. Luke had gotten up at five, just to be sure that he was dressed, had breakfast and was first in line. Even Matthew couldn't believe his eyes.

The trip was long and many of the others nodded off, if they were far enough away from Luke, who insisted on reading from brochures on Bath and Blackbeard.

"You must have bought every book in "Teach's Hole," complained Harold, adjusting his glasses "We could have saved ourselves a lot of time if we had just stayed at camp and let him read all this stuff to us."

"Let him read," urged Haley. "If it wasn't this, he'd find another way to annoy us. At least it keeps him occupied."

Lauren looked suspiciously at the serene look on Haley's face, until she saw the earphone running from her ear to the ipod in her lap. Luke had been babbling on for half an hour and she hadn't heard a word of it!

In another hour the bus pulled to a stop at the visitor's center at Bath, where Jim Hawkins was waiting for them. He was decked out in a colorful eighteenth-century pirate's costume, from a cutlass to an eyepatch over his right eye.

"Aaarggh! Welcome, me hearties!" growled Hawkins in a booming voice. "I be Captain Hawkins, and I sailed with the notorious pirate, Edward Teach, better known to the world as Blackbeard. I was one o' three men he chose as a captain to command a fleet o' three ships. My ship was the *Esperanza*, said to be named for one o' his fourteen wives. I'm gonna take ye 'round to the places he used to 'haunt' hereabouts."

Hawkins waited for a laugh from the few who got his pun, then continued with his interpretation. "First, let's walk down the street to that little red house on the corner. That was where Blackbeard lived with his wife Mary Ormond." When the group got to the front door, Hawkins paused. "Now, look see, at the initials carved on the stone step. It clearly says 'E.T.' That be for Edward Teach. It be a fact that no less than Governor Eden himself performed the wedding ceremony.

"Blackbeard lived here for awhile, trying to retire from bein' a pirate, and live like a respectable gentleman. He and his wife had a carriage for visitin' the local gentry, who considered him a prominent citizen . . . "

"Even though he was a pirate?" asked a skeptical Luke.

"He never robbed none o' them," replied Hawkins, "and he could be quite a charmin' gentleman when he wanted to be. And just like now, money buys influence. And he had a sloop on which he and his missus would sail around, visitin' all the plantations, goin' to balls and . . . "

"When did he ever go pirating?" interrupted Matthew.

"I'm comin' to that, jest be patient, young feller," said Hawkins, but he did not appear to be irritated. "Well, it seems he jest couldn't git 'pirating' as you call it, outta his system. He went back to raidin' up and down the coast, even to Philadelphia, they say. But he never got back to Bath, 'cause Lt. Maynard caught him down at Ocracoke and killed him."

At this point, Hawkins went into a description of the final battle with Blackbeard, which made Dave's version by the fire sound like a nursery story. For once, Luke and Matthew kept quiet, not wanting to miss a single word.

After touring the house, Hawkins invited everyone to board the tram he drove. He kept up a running commentary on the countryside until he turned down a sandy road and parked under a huge oak tree.

"Now somethin' for the ladies in the group. You been mighty patient, so I'll show you a tree where Teach courted Martha Piver, called 'Blackbeard's Oak.'

"I thought he was married to Mary Ormond," said Haley.

"Lord, child," laughed Hawkins, "he married a woman in every port he visited. And many aboard his ship. But they say he was real partial to Martha Piver. He promised to divorce Mary and live with Martha when he returned from his last voyage. But, as we know he didn't return. They say he proposed to her under this very tree."

"Well, at last something of interest to us," whispered Haley. Hawkins cast a quick glance at her and chuckled.

Karen gathered them around her when the tram returned to Bath. "Captain Hawkins says he has a special treat for us. He's going to take us to 'Blackbeard's Castle.' It all sounds very mysterious," she said, smiling. "And he promises that it will be something we will never forget."

It was dark when the group approached a large house with twin turrets. Hawkins looked around slyly, then softly knocked on the door. Eventually, a smaller door placed within the larger one opened, and Hawkins whispered, "Death to Spottswood." The small door closed and the larger one slowly opened. A man wearing eighteenth century clothes stepped aside and waved them in. The group of ten, including Karen, was ushered to a table in a room off of the main dining room. The room was that of an early American tavern, lit by smoking lanterns. The main room was obviously for ordinary tourists, but the rectangular room in which the campers sat seemed to be for special guests.

After dinner, Hawkins stood up and dramatically clapped his hands for silence. "We end the evening with a special ceremony that is not shared with just anyone," he said in a subdued tone. "It is known as 'Blackbeard's Pledge.' " With that he resumed his seat, as the campers looked at one another in eager, yet somewhat apprehensive, anticipation.

A door slowly opened and a huge, bearded man with long, shaggy black hair entered the room, which suddenly seemed smaller for his huge presence. He stretched forth his hands, in which he held a silver cup, with two handles and embossed with carved images worn smooth from much use. He stood at the head of the table and set the cup on it in front of him. He lifted an earthen jug from the table and poured an amber liquid into the cup.

"Now you must take Blackbeard's Pledge," entoned the giant in a deep voice. "Say the words, 'Death to Spottswood,' and drink from the cup. Then pass it on to the person next to you." He handed the cup to the girl seated to his right. Lauren noticed that her voice shook and her hands trembled as she spoke the pledge and drank. The girl then passed the cup to the boy seated to her right.

When Matthew took the cup, he noticed the barely legible carved words on its lip: "Deth to Spottswoode." He drank and handed it to Luke, who accepted it almost reverently. He drank deeply, and only reluctantly passed it on. The giant took it from the last camper on his left, raised it on high, then solemnly turned and walked back through the door from which he came.

Karen eventually broke the spell by calling for the check.

As the others wearily climbed back on the bus, Sailor Hawkins clapped a hand on both Luke and Matthew's shoulders. "I'll tell ye, I don't know that I've ever had any two more enthusiastic lads on me tour," he said. "Ye barely let me get a word in edgewise."

"We're sorry if we kept interrupting you," apologized Matthew. "But we were jam-packed with information before we came." He shot a look at Luke.

"Don't think a thing about it, boy," replied Hawkins. "It was good to have somebody that interested in me old stories. I should sign ye two on as my assistants." He paused for a moment, eyeing the boys sharply and rubbing his chin. "Ye know, I may just have an idea. How would ye like to help me out?"

"How?" asked Matthew.

"I been working with fellers from the University who want to find the remains of *Queen Anne's Revenge*. They think they know where she went down and want to dive down to get relics off her."

"Blackbeard's ship!" exclaimed Luke. "Wow! How can we help?"

"Well, they've chartered me boat to carry their group and their equipment," said Hawkins. "And it seems somebody told 'em nobody knew more about Blackbeard than yours truly." He smiled expansively and stuck out his chest. "Maybe I can work it out with yer counselors for ye to go along with me one day."

"Really?" gushed Luke. "You mean you'd let us go out with you?"

"Sure, lad," laughed Hawkins. "It'd be a shame to waste all that knowledge."

"You have a deal," said Matthew. "We'll ask Dave."

All the way back on the bus, Haley and Lauren kept looking at Luke, puzzled by the gleeful look on his face. Finally, they wormed the story out of him.

"Great, it sounds like we'll have a good time," said Haley.

"What?" Luke looked stunned.

"Well, of course we'll have to go along."

"But . . . but you don't care anything about Blackbeard!" sputtered Luke. "Why would you want to go?"

"Oh, I don't care anything about your old pirate," said Lauren. "But I've always wanted to go skin diving. Mom and Dad let me take a course at the YWCA last year."

"They won't let you dive," said Matthew.

"No," replied Lauren, "but at least I can watch."

"And I've always wanted to go out on a boat," added Haley.

"No girls allowed!" shouted Luke.

"Dave will have to get our parents' permission, and if we say it's too dangerous, they'll say no." Haley smiled impishly.

"That's blackmail!" gasped Luke.

"Well, I guess it will be okay," said Matthew, acknowledging defeat. "If they let us go, they'll have to let you go, too. And you're not too bad—for girls."

"Our pirate adventure spoiled by girls!" said Luke. He stared out the window, baffled by the world's injustice.

"Just think of us as Anne Bonney and Rachel Wall," said Lauren, looking over at Haley's smug smile.

Chapter 4

Boats and Dreamboats

It took all of the kids' persuasive talents to convince Dave to call their parents and ask permission for them to go out on a fishing boat, and only then when one of the adult counselors promised to go. The campers had grown tired of camp routine and sightseeing in the first week, and with three weeks to go, any reasonable diversion came as a blessing. So, the campers split up into small groups geared to particular interests. Even so, the children's participation was conditional upon a carefully-supervised boating safety course.

On the morning that they were to go out with Captain Hawkins, the children waited impatiently at the camp gate for Hawkins' ramshackle truck to pull up. As they boarded, they gave in to their celebrity status among some of their new friends by waving and shouting goodbyes with perhaps too much enthusiasm.

"Boy, will they be green with envy when we come back tonight!" said Matthew.

"Yeah, and loaded down with pirate treasure!" added Luke.

"I really doubt they'll let you keep any treasure," scoffed Lauren.

"And besides, dives like this take a long time—*if* they find anything," chimed in Haley.

"Since when did a girl become such an expert on treasure hunting?" sneered Luke.

"We saw a video at school in social studies about the search for the *U.S.S. Monitor*, smarty," retorted Haley, turning to smile at Karen, who had agreed to go on the day trip. Karen gave her a thumbs-up sign.

"Okay, okay, forget it," said Luke, sulkily realizing that it was useless to argue with a girl about anything important.

A half hour later they were standing on the dock where Hawkins' fishing boat, the *Arabella*, was moored. A man was unloading crates from a small moving van and placing them onto the boat.

A tall, dark-haired man walked toward the group. "Good morning, Captain Hawkins," he said cheerfully. "As you can see, we're right on time." He looked at the youngsters curiously. "Who are these folks?"

"These are my assistants from Camp Ocracoke," said Hawkins. "They know almost as much about Blackbeard as I do. I thought they'd get a kick outta seein' a real live deep-sea treasure hunt up close."

"Hi, kids, I'm Bob Melton," said the young man. "I'm on the history faculty at the University of North Carolina at Chapel Hill. Welcome to the search for the *Queen Anne's Revenge*, but I don't know that we'll find what you would call 'treasure.' "

"I don't approve of children accompanying us," said a deep voice behind them.

They turned to see a stout man of medium height and grey hair and beard. His face was shaded by a wide straw hat and his eyes were hidden behind large sunglasses.

"Captain Hawkins, meet Dr. John Anderson," said Bob. "He's on the faculty of the Archaeology Department at the University of North Carolina at Greensboro. The campuses are collaborating on this project, and Dr. Anderson is a specialist on underwater archaeology."

"They'll be fine," protested Hawkins. "They're good kids, and I thought it would be a real treat for 'em."

"The insurance policy for the project only covers equipment, not people. Especially not unauthorized juveniles," said Anderson huffily.

"The camp has agreed to accept full responsibility for their conduct and safety," said Karen. "And their parents gave verbal permission to take the trip. I assure you, they won't get in your way."

"You know, Dr. Anderson, we're filming the expedition," added Bob. "Some footage for the press relating to interest in the project by school age children could be very useful publicity. It was hard enough to come up with the limited funds we received."

Anderson pursed his lips as he glanced at the photographer, the children and Melton. Finally he said, "Okay, but I count on this young lady and the Captain to make sure they don't interfere with our work."

"Great!" shouted Hawkins, not giving anyone time for second thoughts. "Let's get aboard." He guided everyone up the short gangplank to the deck of his boat. Under the cabin roof were several metal casings with delicate-looking dials and meters, and a small monitor attached to a computer. "Those are mighty impressive gadgets you've got there, Dr. Melton," said Hawkins, trying to stay out of the way of a technician who was monitoring some gauges.

"Call me Bob" said Melton. "It's hardly state-of-the-art, but it was the best we could come up with on short notice. We speeded up the schedule for the project to try to get some diving in before the hurricane season. We received final notice that our funding had been approved just two weeks ago. We're not sure as to the exact location of the wreck, but if we're lucky, this equipment should be adequate to help us locate it."

"This here is the best 'equipment' there is for locatin' old shipwrecks," said Hawkins, tapping the side of his nose. "I've been sailing around these sounds for over thirty years. Lots of ships have gone down in storms, and German subs sank a bunch of 'em durin' World War Two. I could show you where every one of 'em is."

"I bet you can," laughed Melton. Turning to the children, he said, "Captain Hawkins tells me that you all are experts on Blackbeard. Is that right?"

"Us guys," spoke up Luke defensively. "Not the girls. They're just along for the ride."

"Oh, I see," said Bob nodding.

"Some writers think Blackbeard intentionally sank the *Queen Anne's Revenge* offshore, loaded with treasure, rather than burying it on land," said Matthew. "He knew all about the hidden shoals and sandbanks along the coast."

"I can see you fellows know your stuff," said Melton. "Maybe the Captain was wise to bring you along after all. If we get stumped, we'll call on you."

"Cool!" shouted Luke. "Just let us know how we can help."

Looking past the boys, Bob saw Lauren standing by the diving equipment, and Haley peeking over the shoulder of the technician as he adjusted various dials.

"Are you girls interested in all this?" Bob asked, his arm making a sweeping gesture that took in the array of the equipment.

"Oh, Lauren has always been goofy on computers because her father is a computer whiz," said Haley. "But what she really likes is the diving. When she grows up, she's going to be a professional deep-sea diver."

"Well, I'm kinda new at it myself," said Bob, "but I'll see if Dr. Anderson can spare some time to show the gear to you. He's been diving for years and years."

"I don't know," said Lauren. "He didn't seem to like us very much."

"Don't let him frighten you. His bark is worse than his bite."

"Okay, Doc," Hawkins said, addressing Bob, "let's get underway. You just tell me where you want to go first."

"I'll go down to the cabin and consult with Dr. Anderson about his charts. Then I'll come back up and give you the coordinates." He disappeared down the short flight of steps that led to the cabin below.

True to her word, Karen kept the kids on the cushions that ran along the stern. The girls agreed to be still, but it took a great deal more effort to control the boys, particularly Luke. She finally got them to be content with constant rubber-necking as they tried to take in all the activity around them.

After showing Hawkins the first site they wanted to explore, Bob spent most of his time talking with Karen.

"I think he likes her," Lauren confided to Haley.

"Are you kidding?" said Haley. "He's old enough to be her father."

"I heard him tell the Captain that he's only twenty-six," said Lauren. "Besides, I think he's a dreamboat."

"Um," replied a skeptical Haley.

The children were fascinated as Dr. Anderson ordered the boat to anchor in Drum Inlet, then donned scuba diving gear. In no time he had plunged into the water, carrying a small TV camera.

"Come over here, kids," said Bob pointing to a television screen. "In a moment you will see an image on the screen from the underwater camera. It is then downloaded onto the computer. Later, we can extract whatever shots we want for future analysis."

The children watched with rapt attention as images of the ocean bottom appeared on the screen. With infinite patience, Dr. Anderson swept the camera back and forth.

"Wow!" exclaimed Haley. "This is great. See that . . ."

"Hey! That looks like part of a ship." exclaimed Luke. "Maybe that's part of the *Queen Anne's Revenge*!"

They all pressed closer to the screen in eager anticipation. "You're being too anxious, kids," cautioned Bob. "Nine times out of ten what you'll see will be a natural formation on the ocean floor or a modern shipwreck. Deep-sea exploration is a slow process. I'm afraid you'll find it mostly pretty boring stuff."

Sure enough, on closer examination, the image proved to be the hulk of a small freighter. But as Matthew straightened up, a large boat off the port side caught his attention. It was coming to anchor some two hundred yards away.

"Say, who's that?" he asked.

Bob reached for a pair of binoculars, with which he

observed the other boat. "It's just as I suspected," he said, lowering the binoculars. "It's a boat belonging to McBride Salvage. We've had word that they were preparing a search for the *Queen Anne's Revenge*, too."

"Is that a problem?" asked Matthew. "Can't you guys work together?"

"Not really," replied Bob. "They're only interested in recovering gold and silver from the wreck."

"Isn't that what you're after?" asked Luke.

Bob smiled. "If it's there, but our main focus is to recover historical artifacts to research eighteenth century life, then to place it on display to the public in museums. Companies like McBride's often destroy delicate artifacts while looking for treasure. In addition to individual artifacts, we ultimately hope to raise the entire ship, if possible."

"How can you raise up a whole ship that old?" asked Lauren.

"We hope the publicity of the find and a touring display of artifacts will generate enough interest for us to get a grant to hire the necessary equipment. But it will be a long, painstaking procedure, which our friend McBride has no interest in doing."

"Can't you stop him?" questioned Luke.

"No, I'm afraid we can't," said Bob. "The wreck is in deep enough water and so old that it would be declared appropriate for salvage. That makes it a 'first come, first served' deal. If McBride gets to it before us, he has every right to whatever he finds."

"But couldn't you . . . " began Luke. But Bob held up his hand to halt further questions.

"I'd better signal Dr. Anderson to come up," said Bob. "We'll need to talk this over."

He spoke into a microphone that communicated with a headset worn by Anderson.

The children stared silently out at the other boat, which had now taken on the aura of a silent menace.

Chapter 5

Attack at Sea

"Please, Dave, we could do such a good job," begged Haley. "And it would mean so much to us."

Dave sighed heavily. Faced with that sweet, entreating face, he knew he was defeated. "All right," he said. "But Karen will have to chaperone. One bad report from her and the project is cancelled."

"Hooray!" shouted Lauren. "Just wait, Dave, this will be the greatest end-of-camp show you've ever seen. You won't be sorry."

Watching the two girls walk out of his office, Dave had a sneaking suspicion that he was sorry already.

Haley and Lauren ran up to where Matthew and Luke were standing. "It's on!" exclaimed Haley. "Dave said we can use our video camera to make a movie about searching for the *Queen Anne's Revenge*, and get the professors to show whatever they find."

"Yeah," said Luke, his eyes gleaming. "We can call it 'Searching for Lost Treasure.' "

"Relax, Luke, you're not Stephen Spielberg yet," said Haley, smirking.

"There is one problem," said Lauren, looking down at the ground. "I kinda told Lucy about what we planning, and she wants to be a part of it."

"Well, to tell the truth, I spilled the beans to Harold, and he wants in on the deal," said Matthew.

"Oh great," said Luke. "Pretty soon the whole camp will be on board. We gotta . . . ."

"Don't worry," interrupted Matthew. "They'll be the only two, and they'll be our liaisons here at camp."

"Huh?" said Luke.

"You know, kind of like our agents back here to keep track of things," explained Matthew.

"*Secret* agents," demanded Luke.

"Okay, I'll get Karen to call the professors and Captain Hawkins to set the whole thing up," said Lauren. "After all, we've only got three weeks to put this together."

Arrangements had been made for Captain Hawkins to pick up Karen and the kids every morning after camp chores had been done. Luke grumbled about having to rake the grounds and clean up the dining hall, when there was sunken treasure just waiting to be found, but a deal was a deal.

The next morning, as the five of them waited at the camp entrance to be picked up, Lauren added a bit of reality.

"You know, of course, that we only have three weeks. They may not even find the ship, and if they find the ship they may not find any treasure on it."

"That's okay," countered Haley. "We'll have shots of going out on the boat and diving. And we can add pictures of all those places we saw at Bath. We can even dress up the boys as pirates and make a little play about it."

"Don't build it up too big," cautioned Matthew. "If we promise the kids at camp that we've found a treasure, we'll have to deliver. Better have a back up plan, and it'd better be more than a travelogue on the Outer Banks."

"Aw, you guys are nothin' but spoil sports," snorted Luke. "The professors are *gonna* find the ship, and they're *gonna* find a treasure!"

I talked to Bob, and he said he can use his computer to edit the film you shoot into any kind of 'movie' we want to make," said Karen. "So don't worry about having something to entertain the other campers."

Soon a van pulled up at the gate, with Bob at the wheel. "Captain Hawkins asked me to pick you up and bring you to the dock," he said, smiling."I hope you don't mind."

"No, not at all," replied Karen, ushering the kids into the back seats.

As the van drove off, Haley looked at Bob and Karen talking and laughing in the front seat. "It's a good thing that Karen agreed to act as chaperone," she said. "But I'm really surprised."

"Are you kidding?" answered Lauren. "Do you see the way she looks whenever she's around Bob? They're like lovebirds. I think it's *soooo* romantic."

"Good grief," said Matthew, rolling his eyes. Luke stuck his finger down his throat and made gagging noises.

"Boys," sniffed Haley.

"Girls," huffed Luke.

When the van came to a stop at the dock, Dr. Anderson, Captain Hawkins, George the technician, and Andy the photographer were already aboard the *Arabella*. "We've been waiting for over an hour," said Dr. Anderson, sourly.

"I'm sorry, Dr. Anderson," apologized Bob. "We'll be right with you."

As the boat sped out to the previous day's anchorage, With Andy's help, Matthew shot scenes with his video camera, careful to include footage of the technician fiddling with the controls of the electronic equipment and the professors checking their instruments. Captain Hawkins mugged shamelessly in his best "gruff old sailor" pose as he stood at the helm.

"Our film so far is pretty disappointing," said Anderson, pointing to the computer monitor, "but I think we're in the right area, according to the accounts of the testimony that Teach made before the Maritime Commission at the time of the sinking. I'm having Hawkins return to the area where we dove yesterday."

Hours went by as the boat crisscrossed the channel in a grid pattern. Since there was nothing of interest to film, Matthew had put away the camera, and Luke dozed off from boredom. The girls kept themselves amused by noticing how often Karen and Bob seemed to find excuses to help each other with the scientific equipment.

Anderson jolted everyone alert by slapping the technician's shoulder as each stared into the monitor. "That looks very promising, George. Get a fix on that location so Bob and I can go down for a closer look."

Suddenly Matthew shaded his eyes and squinted into the distance. "There they are again," he said.

Everyone saw a boat bearing the name of "McBride Salvage" come to anchor about two hundred yards away.

"Oh, brother," said Luke. "Now they're gonna horn in on our party."

"Not if we can help it," said Dr. Anderson softly. "According to the charts we're near the Atlantic shelf. If what Teach testified is accurate, his ship could not have been that far out. They will be wasting their time in deep-water investigation. Let's just keep a low profile and act as if we haven't found anything interesting, shall we?"

Sure enough, before long the larger boat was hoisting a deep-sea vehicle alongside and lowering it into the water.

A satisfied smile played across Anderson's face. "That's what McBride gets for not being more of a scholar. From where he's looking it's clear that he has contented himself with the newspaper accounts of the time concerning the sinking. He didn't bother to pore over the records of the Maritime Commission. He'll never find anything out there."

Dr. Anderson was so anxious to get into the water that he bustled around the deck, hustling everyone aside as he donned oxygen tank, mask and flippers. For all his jests at his rival's error, he kept glancing at the other boat.

Finally in exasperation he stormed out, "If you children don't get out of the way, you'll not be allowed on this boat again, publicity or no publicty!" His glare was so intimidating the kids shrank away to the safety of the cushions at the stern. Joining her, Luke muttered something about the doctor looking like an elephant seal in his black diving suit.

After Bob and Anderson disappeared under the water, everyone crowded around the computer monitor as images from the underwater camera appeared. They could barely see the ocean floor and two black blurs, which George, the technician, identified as the divers.

"I can't see anything," complained Luke.

"Don't worry, I'll make an adjustment," said George. After fine-tuning a dial for a few moments, the black and white image sharpened. "There we go. You'll get used to identifiying objects without the aid of a color monitor."

As if they were one body, the kids leaned forward while the camera focused in on a shape that was some kind of wooden ship. But the next scene was of Dr. Anderson's head shaking back and forth. The only other thing to appear was a cylindrical object about five feet long buried in the sand. After forty minutes, they could see Dr. Anderson jerking his thumb up toward the surface, and the screen became fuzzy, then went black..

Waiting for the men to surface, Matthew heard the sound of a motor surging loudly toward the *Arabella*. He looked up to see an outboard boat swinging into the area where the bubbles from Bob and Dr. Anderson's oxygen tank were appearing.

"That boat is going to hit the professors!" he yelled.

The Prakkes began frantically waving their arms and shouting, trying to attract the attention of the pilot of the approaching boat.

"What is it?" asked Karen, coming up to the kids.

"Bob and Dr. Anderson are in trouble!" shouted Luke.

Just as two heads bobbed to the surface, the outboard swerved, sending a large wave that engulfed the divers. Lauren and Haley held their breath as the camera was wrenched out of Bob's hands. He made a lunge to grab it, but it sank beneath the surface. As he was preparing to descend for it, the surging water tore the mouthpiece from his lips. Bob's thrashing arms indicated that he was unable to get his breath. As his head disappeared beneath the water, Dr. Anderson grabbed Bob, turned him onto his back and swam back toward the *Arabella*.

Karen and George helped Bob slowly ascend the ladder.

He came aboard and stretched full-length onto the deck, spluttering and gasping for breath. Anderson followed and knelt beside his colleague, a worried look on his face.

"Bob, are you all right?" he said.

Bob could not answer, but he nodded and struggled to sit up. After several deep breaths he said, "Yes . . . I'm all right. Thanks to you, Doctor."

"From what the kids said, you could have been killed!" said Karen. Her hand rested gently upon Bob's shoulder.

"Not very dignified, I'm afraid," Bob said, but he did not shrug off Karen's hand.

"I'm sorry about the camera," said Bob. "We can get it on another dive. At least we have the film in the computer. Let's head back to shore."

"Well, I'm reportin' those guys to the Coast Guard," vowed Hawkins. "No room on the water for such things."

In an hour they had docked and Bob and Dr. Anderson emerged from the cabin after changing into street clothes. Everyone piled into the van and drove to the Coast Guard station at Buxton. As they parked the van, Matthew pointed out a truck with "McBride Salvage" painted on the door.

"Seems McBride has beat us to it," mused Anderson.

When the group entered the doorway, a uniformed officer looked at them and said, "Ladies and gentlemen, please have a seat. Mr. McBride was just reporting an unfortunate incident in which you were involved."

"There was no 'unfortunate incident,' " Dr. Anderson snapped. "This man's employees tried to run us down in the water with their boat!"

"You're wrong," McBride protested . "My assistants were trying to get some prospective film shots of our salvage area. When they saw that there were divers in the area, they veered off to avoid hitting them. Since there were no bouys in the water, it was an understandable mistake."

"That's a lie!" said Lauren hotly. "There were so bouys in the water. Any idiot could have seen them!" Karen put her hand on Lauren's shoulder and pulled her back, just when it seemed she was going to attack the man.

"This is certainly an awkward situation. It seems we have a difference of opinion as to what happened, and witnesses on both sides asserting opposite points of view," said the officer, who identified himself as Lieutenant Stewart. "I will report the incident to headquarters and let them make a judgment if anyone is guilty of negligence. In the meantime, since both parties have valid permits to be in the area, all I can do is urge you both to exercise extreme caution and observe the rules of the sea in your endeavors. I will add, however, that my men will make a special effort to keep you under observation to make certain nothing like this happens in the future."

"I still want to lodge a formal complaint to the magistrate's office," said Dr. Anderson.

"Very well, sir," said Lieutenant Stewart. "I will take your statement. As for you, Mr. McBride, I think it best if you and your men leave at this time."

"Yes, I agree that would be best," said McBride. Turning to Bob, he said, "I hope you will accept my profound apology, Dr. Melton." His tone was polite, but the look in his eyes was unmistakably threatening.

Matthew saw Bob's hand ball into a fist, and he thought he was going to hit McBride. But the professor just shoved his fist into his pocket and glared silently at the man.

Once outside, Karen and Bob began to protest against the position of the Coast Guard regarding the incident, but Dr. Anderson raised his hand to silence them.

"We've lodged a formal complaint," he said. "There's more important work to do. I know it's getting late in the day and these children need to get back to camp, but I want to download the film from the computer and take it back to the lab. I think we'll find something very interesting on it."

Puzzled but interested in Dr. Anderson's comment, the kids were impatient as they all drove back to the *Arabella*, downloaded the film onto a CD, and drove to the beach house where Dr. Anderson and Bob were staying. The "lab" was nothing more than a spare bedroom with another computer and other equipment.

"Now, then, ladies and gentlemen, take a seat and let's see what we've got here." For once, Dr. Anderson spoke in a soft tone, decidedly different from his customary deep growl. He started the CD and quickly advanced it for several minutes. Then he played it backward and forward, stroking his beard and muttering excitedly to himself.

"Aha, that's it! Come here and look, all of you, and tell me what you see."

The Prakkes, Bob and Karen crowded around the monitor. There seemed to be an endless expanse of ocean sand, which appeared to float due to the sunlight streaming down through the rippling water. Finally, a cylinder appeared, buried in the sand. Matthew recognized it as the same object he had seen on the monitor aboard the *Arabella*.

"What are we supposed to be looking at?" asked Haley.

"This is a debris field," said Dr. Anderson, pointing to various objects covered by sand. "If we're lucky, the objects you see on the ocean floor will be from the *Queen Anne's Revenge*. And if we're *very* lucky, it will lead us to the wreck herself." He sat back in his chair, a rare smile spreading across his face.

"So we're about to find the treasure?" asked Luke.

"Well, as a scientist, I'd have to say it's too soon to tell," said Dr. Anderson."

But as a sure-enough 'treasure hunter,' I'm tempted to say you may be right," added Bob.

"Yes!" shouted Luke, raising his fist into the air.

Chapter 6

A Mysterious Intruder

"I'm sorry, kids, but we just can't take a chance on your being hurt."

The Prakkes stared in mute disbelief at Dave as he gave them the bad news from behind his desk at the camp office. Karen stood beside him, looking sympathetically at them.

"But you don't know that the boat meant to come so close to us," pleaded Matthew.

"Or that it would ever happen again," chimed in Haley.

"That is true," said Dave, "but I said that if we believed you might be in any danger, we'd have to call a halt to this project. Besides, it was outside of camp jurisdiction from the beginning. There's still time for you to find another project topic."

The four youngsters walked out of the office and sat glumly on the front steps.

"There goes our pirate adventure!" pouted Luke.

"I don't know," said Lauren.

"What do you mean?" said Haley.

"We owe it to Bob and Karen—even Dr. Anderson—to help them any way we can to promote this project, particularly after they've been so nice to us," continued Lauren. "And most of all, we can't let those jerks stand in the way of true love."

"Or finding pirate treasure!" chortled Luke.

"Okay," said Matthew, "we're with you, but what did you have in mind?

Two hours later, they piled out of the camp jeep that went daily to collect the mail and supplies in Ocracoke. They waved to Fred, a counselor, promising to be back at five.

"I guess our goose is cooked if Dave finds out what we've done," said Matthew.

"I left a note for Karen," replied Lauren. "She'll cover for us, especially when I bring her a note from Bob."

"I wouldn't count on 'true love' too much, if I were you," said Matthew skeptically.

"So what's the plan again?" asked Haley.

"Matthew said he was filming when the boat almost hit us, right?" said Lauren. "Well, if we give that tape to the Coast Guard, then Mr. McBride's permit will be withdrawn and they won't have the right to be in the inlet anymore, and we can go back to being on Captain Hawkins' boat with the expedition because we won't be in danger anymore."

"Why didn't you give it to them yesterday?" asked Luke.

"I left it on the boat in all the excitement," confessed Matthew sheepishly.

"Okay, but if we're going to do it, let's go," said Haley. "We've got to be at the post office before five."

The group made its way to the dock, where they found the *Arabella*'s berth empty.

"I guess we'll have to wait until they get back," said Luke, disappointed. "Too bad we couldn't have called them."

"Maybe Captain Hawkins put it in his office for safe-keeping," suggested Matthew. "Let's go over and see if we can find it."

Standing in front of the darkened office, they resigned themselves to wait the long hours until the Captain's return.

"Why don't we see if the door's open and look around?" suggested Luke. "I bet the Captain won't mind."

"That's breaking and entering," said Haley. "Besides, he wouldn't go off and leave the door unlocked."

"It's not a crime if it's open," countered Luke. He immediately turned the knob and pushed the door open. With a florish he waved the others in, smiling. Haley and Lauren made a big show of ignoring his victory.

The little office was a mess. There was only one small desk and two chairs, but boxes of old advertising brochures and charts were piled up everywhere. An open door led to an adjoining storage room.

"Who'd think a place this small could hold all this junk," observed Luke.

"Here it is!" exclaimed Lauren, triumphantly holding up the small camera. "It was under a pile of papers on the desk."

They turned out the light and were just leaving when they heard footsteps on the small porch outside.

"I didn't think they'd get back so soon," said Matthew. "Let's tell them what we have in mind."

"It's not them," hissed Lauren. "It looks like one of the men that was on McBride's boat!"

"Hide, quick!" said Luke.

The four just had time to squeeze behind the desk before the door opened. In the semi-darkness of the office they saw a shadowy figure enter, look around, then make for the door that led to the storage room

The kids looked at each other as they heard objects being moved around in the other room.

"Maybe we ought to . . . " began Haley.

"Shhh!" said Matthew. "He's coming back."

They held their breaths for what seemed an eternity as the figure crept across the room, opened the door and left.

"What do you suppose he wanted?" asked Lauren.

"I dunno, but he couldn't have been up to any good," observed Luke.

"Let's wait outside for Captain Hawkins and Bob," suggested Matthew. "Maybe they'll have an idea. At any rate, they should know what happened."

It was shortly after four o'clock before the Captain's old truck pulled up in front of the office. Bob, the Captain and Dr. Anderson emerged with surprised looks.

"Well, what brings you here?" asked Hawkins "Karen called and said Dave didn't want you to come back."

"Captain! Bob!" exclaimed Lauren. "Somebody came into your office and went through your things!"

"Whoa! What's all this?" Hawkins asked, holding up his hands.

The four of them began speaking at once. Despite the jumble of excited voices, the three men finally got an idea as to what had occurred.

"Well, I'll just go out back and have a look around," said Hawkins, striding into the other room.

While he was gone, the kids told Bob and Dr. Anderson about their plan, holding up the camera.

"There's a video player in the storage room," said Bob. "Let's put the tape in and look at it—that is, if your thief didn't take it."

"I don't think he was carrying anything when he left," said Matthew. "And he's not *our* thief. It was one of the McBride Salvage crew."

"I'm sorry," replied Bob. "I didn't mean to offend you."

Hawkins was just putting some diving tanks aside when they joined him. "I've looked at everything, and I can't find anything missing," he said.

"Not even the video player and monitor?" asked Dr. Anderson

"No, I guess he didn't see it," answered Hawkins.

The kids waited eagerly as Bob put the tape into the machine and turned on the monitor. Images of the preparations for the dive flashed onto the screen, and the salvage ship at anchor in the distance. Then a series of squiggled lines appeared, followed by a dark screen.

"Matthew!" screamed Haley and Lauren. "What happened?"

"I must have accidentally hit the erase button in all the excitement," said Matthew dolefully.

"Great! There goes our evidence," scoffed Luke.

"Don't worry about it, kids," said Bob, gently. "I don't think we'll have any more trouble with those guys. It was just a foolish stunt on their part. And besides, I have good news for you."

"What?" asked Haley.

"Karen was so upset with your disappointment in Dave's

office that she went back to talk to him. She convinced him to let you continue with the project, but you'll have to stay on land from now on."

"Hooray!" shouted Lauren and Haley.

But Luke would not be mollified. "That's no fun. I wanted to be out there when you bring up the treasure."

"Well, you can help us count all those thousands of gold coins here in the office," Bob said, patting him on the arm.

"What about the intruder?" asked Matthew.

"I think you have an overactive imagination," said Dr. Anderson curtly. "I don't think McBride would do that."

"I think it was just one of the beach bums that hang around here," said Hawkins. "More'n likely he wanted to pick up something he could sell at a pawn shop for some quick cash. Guess he couldn't find anythin' to sell. Just be glad he wasn't a hardened criminal; he might have cut yer throat." He smiled wickedly as he drew a finger across his throat.

"Oh, Captain!" said Lauren. Her thoughts were somewhere between irritation at his joke and the realization that he had described the very fate they may have escaped.

"Did you go down to the debris field?" asked Luke.

"Not today," said Bob. "Dr. Anderson and I spent the day checking equpment and writing a progress report."

"I thought you were so hot about it," said Luke.

"First we have to convince our funding agency of what we have found. As a matter of fact, we just stopped by to make some prints from the tape of yesterday's dive. With what we've compiled, the University Board of Trustees just might give us an extension on our stay here."

"Hey, it's almost five," shouted Matthew. "We'd better get over to the post office. No sense getting into trouble just when we've gotten a reprieve."

They ran out the door and raced each other to the jeep parked outside, filled with supplies. They scrambled aboard as Fred shot them mock scowls of disapproval, then headed the vehicle toward camp.

Chapter 7

The Ghost Appears

Luke tossed and turned, unable to sleep because of the heat. Suddenly he had the bright idea of sneaking out and taking a shower. Despite himself, he had to be amazed at his brilliance!

He dragged a sleepy Matthew out of bed and they crept between the rows of bunks, pausing whenever someone made a noise. They froze when a voice mumbled in the darkness, then realized that Harold talked in his sleep! Boy, was he going to get razzed in the morning. After slowly opening the screen door to prevent it from squeaking, they quickly descended the three steps of the cabin.

"Why don't we wake up the girls?" asked Matthew.

"Okay," agreed Luke, "but I think you're nuts."

Scratches on the screen and irritable whispers finally brought the girls out. The four made their way down the path to the showers.

Luke was just noticing how pleasantly cool it was under the trees by the shower house, when he spotted—something—from the corner of his eye. Squinting into the darkness, he tried to make out what had caught his attention. A light. The reflection of the lighthouse? A passing airplane?

"There it is again!" said Luke.

"What?" asked Lauren.

Perhaps he should have ignored it, but Luke had the reputation of being too curious for his own good. Intrigued, He cautiously continued down the trail, pausing now and then to listen. Nothing. He crept forward, stopping again as he detected a strange odor. It smelled like smoke and something else. Sulphur?

"Where are you going?" said Haley.

Luke ignored his sister as he approached the sand dunes where the counselors always held the campfire meetings. Were they having one now? If so, he would make a big deal of it at the next group meeting. Imagine them having that kind of fun without telling the campers about it!

But the light didn't seem like a campfire, and the odor was not like wood smoke. What, then, could it be?

The others caught up to Luke when he stopped to look in the direction of a movement off to his right, on a large sand dune about thirty yards away. "Look at that!" whispered Luke.

The moon was full tonight and he was certain he could see a figure on the dune. In the moonlight they all saw something that made the hair stand up on the back of their necks.

A man, well over six feet, stood dressed in an eighteenth century coat, knee breeches and a tricorner hat. Across his chest was a bandoleer containing several pistols, and in his right hand he was brandishing a huge cutlass.

But what captured their attention was the full black beard and the shaggy black hair under his hat, from which smouldering ropes caused his head to be wreathed in smoke.

It was Blackbeard!

The apparition turned to look at them. Suddenly from the twisted mouth came a horrible, evil laugh that seemed to rebound from the surrounding dunes.

As one, they turned and raced across the sand. Only once did Luke slacken his pace to look over his shoulder, and he wished he hadn't. The figure was slashing the air with his mighty sword and descending the dune in their direction!

Their legs ached from the pull of the sand, and their lungs seemed to be on the point of bursting, but none dared stop running.. Indeed, all of them were certain that they were on the verge of being whisked away to some awful place or slaughtered on the spot by that terrifying spectre on the beach!

If the stones and pine burrs had bothered his bare feet before, this time Luke took no notice of them as he sped down the path under the trees. He could no longer smell that horrible odor of sulphur, nor hear that frightening laugh. If only they could make it to the cabin, somehow he felt they would be safe!

There was the cabin, standing like a silent sentinel in the moonlight. The other campers were there, and they would protect him and the others. And he could warn them of their own impending doom.

The Prakkes lept the three steps in a single bound and burst through the screen door. Lights blazed forth and a gaggle of startled voices rent the darkness.

"Help! Help!" screamed Luke. "Don't let him get us!"

Luke dived onto his bunk, while Matthew and the girls babbled in incomprehensible gasps of what they had seen.

Harold blinked against the sudden light, then grabbed Matthew by the shoulders and shook him. "What's the matter with you, man? Have you gone nuts?"

"I saw him, Harold!" stammered Matthew. "It was Blackbeard, big as life—bigger—and he was coming right at us!"

"What's he yelling about?" said one of the boys who had clustered into a tight knot around Luke's bunk.

"I dunno," answered another. "He's blabbering something about Blackbeard."

Fred strode quickly over from his bunk at the other end of the cabin, pushing the boys aside. "What's going on here? Are you guys fighting?"

"No, Fred," said Harold. "The Prakkes sneaked out and thought they saw the ghost of Blackbeard."

"Was he lookin' for his head?" snicked a boy.

"Don't be a jerk!" snapped Lauren. "We all saw it."

Fred took each of the Prakkes in turn by the shoulders "It's okay, you guys. You were just imagining things. That's what you get for leaving after lights out. You were just lucky you didn't get hurt out in the woods after dark. You girls go back to your cabin and report to Karen. That settles it, I'm putting a deadbolt lock on the door to keep everyone in."

"No, Fred," gasped Luke, "We really saw Blackbeard. He was out there on the dunes and he was coming to get us!" He was going to get the girls to confirm his story, but he saw that they had already left.

"Calm down, Luke," said Fred. "Here, put your head between your knees. Somebody get a paper bag he can breathe into." When Luke had done as Fred ordered, and had settled down, the counselor faced the group. "Is everyone accounted for? I swear, if anybody has been playing pranks, when I get through with them, what Luke is going through will seem like a picnic by comparison."

"Nobody's missing, Fred," said one of the boys. "Honest, none of us are pulling any stunts."

"Yeah, that's what he gets for reading those books of his, and talking about pirates and ghosts all the time," said another boy. "He always made a big deal about there being no such thing as ghosts. Not so smart-alecky now, is he?"

Matthew balled his fist to threaten Luke's heckler, who retreated behind some other boys.

Slowly, Fred got the boys back to their bunks and turned off the light. He offered to let Luke switch bunks with the boy next to his own, but Luke said he was okay and wanted to stay with his cousin.

As he lay in his bunk, experiencing an occasional shiver, like an aftershock, Luke wished he had Matthew's calm nature. His cousin had already recovered his composure. As he was thinking these thoughts, he heard Matthew's voice in the dark.

"Sure you're okay, Luke? Do you think it was just a mirage we saw?"

"No, Matthew," replied Luke. "Whatever it was out there was no mirage. You saw it too, didn't you?"

"Yeah," replied Matthew. "It was real."

Chapter 8

Humiliation

The next day the four Prakkes had to endure the taunts of their fellow campers, as well as stern warnings from the counselors about sneaking out at night. It was only Karen's intervention that kept them from being grounded for the remainder of their time at the camp. "But no more of this 'looking for Blackbeard's ship' nonsense," entoned Dave. "Do you understand me?"

Even the irrepressible Luke was silent, but Lauren was already formulating a plan to continue working with the professors.

Outside the counselors' office Harold and Lucy were waiting for them.

"So, are you all going to have to walk the plank?" asked Harold, dodging the poorly aimed fist that Luke directed to his arm.

"Well, at least you can do stuff with us around camp," said Lucy. "We haven't seen much of you in the last few days," she added significantly.

Their friend's comment was not lost on the Prakkes. "We're sorry, it's just that we got so wrapped up in the search that we forgot all about anything else," apologized Lauren. "But if you really want to help, there is something you can do for us."

"Uh oh," said Haley, shaking her head. "I've seen that look lots of times before, and it's not good news for anybody. Just what are you planning now to get us into trouble? And our friends, too."

"They said they wanted to be with us, didn't they?" said Lauren. "And the only way they can be with us is to help us get back on the search project, right? Besides, I am sick of everybody making fun of us about last night."

Just then, several campers walked past them. "Seen any more ghosts, you guys?" one asked.

"Yeah, better be careful or Blackbeard's gonna getcha," added another. They all walked off, laughing uproariously.

Luke turned to look meaningfully at his sister. "Okay," Haley said, "you win the argument. You're going to grow up to be a good lawyer, like Dad."

"What's first on the schedule?" asked Matthew, surrendering his accustomed leadership role of the group.

"We've got to get Karen back on our team," said Haley. "And we've got to pool our money to do it. So cough up your spending money."

"Why?" asked Luke.

"For the flowers, silly," replied Haley.

"Huh?" said Matthew and Luke together.

"Oh, I see," said Lauren, smiling. "Good plan, girl."

"What are you two talking about?" asked Luke.

"Boys, they never have a clue," said Haley, contemptuously. "Honestly!"

The six walked toward the pay telephone hanging on the wall of the dining hall building. Matthew, Luke and Harold handed over all of their spare change and followed the girls, scratching their heads and looking at each other.

At 2:00 Karen and the four Prakkes joined Dr. Anderson and Bob outside the City Hall building. Karen beamed as she greeted Bob.

"Thank you for the roses, they were lovely. But you shouldn't have."

Bob stared at her for a moment and was about to speak, when he saw the look on Lauren and Haley's faces.

"Oh . . . you're welcome. I just thought I'd show my appreciation for all you and the kids have done."

"I don't know what we've done," replied Karen. "As a matter of fact, I thought I was going to lose my job this morning when I told Dave that I had to bring the kids down here for the hearing on our complaint."

"Well, I guess we'd better go in," said Dr. Anderson. "The magistrate is expecting us."

They all filed into the front door, with Bob holding it open. He smiled as Lauren walked past him, winking in a conspiratorial way.

The group walked down a narrow hallway to a glass door marked "Magistrate's Office." Again, Bob held the door open as they entered and sat in a row of chairs arranged in front of a small desk. Seated behind the desk was a thin, balding man with wire-rimmed glasses. In a chair across the room sat the County Sheriff in a chair that was far too small to accommodate his considerable girth. In the row behind them was seated McBride and two associates.

"Now, we have the matter of *Anderson v. McBride*," said the magistrate. "According to the complaint, the plaintiff alleges that employees of the McBride Salvage Company operated a motorboat in the immediate vicinity of two divers, to wit, Dr. David Anderson and Dr. Robert Melton, in such a manner as to make them liable to the charge of reckless endangerment. Does that sum up the situation, Sheriff?"

"Yes, sir," replied the corpulent law officer.

"The defendants, Mr. Charles Hester and Mr. Arthur Johnson, employees of the McBride Salvage Company, deny the charges, stating that the divers were in no danger from the boat they were operating, and further, that there were no marker bouys indicating that there were divers in the area." This time the Sheriff merely nodded. "And the only witnesses were four minors on board a vessel captained by one James Hawkins, under charter by the plaintiffs."

When the Sheriff nodded again, the magistrate had Dr. Anderson and Bob give their side of the story, then heard the counter-argument from Hester and Johnson. Finally, he had each of the Prakkes give their testimony.

"Now, as I understand it, Sheriff,, you were called to the

YMCA camp last night to investigate an alleged trespasser at the camp?"

"Yes, your honor," said the Sheriff, rising for the first time. "The four children standing over there claimed to have seen someone on the beach. My deputy and I investigated, but could find no evidence of any trespasser. We talked to the adminstrators of the camp, because the kid were in bed, but they could not give us much information. We returned to the office and filed a report."

"Who did the children say trespassed at the camp?"

"It was a pirate, sir," answered the Sheriff, looking distinctly uncomfortable. "A pirate ghost."

"A ghost?" asked the magistrate, looking up for the first time. It was all Luke could do not to burst out laughing at the incredulous look on the official's face.

"Yes, sir, that's what the children said."

The magistrate ordered the Prakkes to stand up. "Do any of you wish to add anything to your story about last night?"

The kids looked at each other, then Matthew turned back to the magistrate. "No, sir, we don't," he said.

"Do you wish to amend your testimony regarding the incident on the ocean the other day?"

"No, sir," answered Matthew.

The magistrate stared down at the papers on his desk for several moments, then looked up sternly at the Prakkes. "It is a serious charge made against the McBride Salvage Company, based largely on your testimony. And it is equally serious to waste the time of the police to investigate what is undoubtedly a prank on your part. This court could deal severely with you over these matters, both of which clearly stem from the overactive imagination of bored children. But I will let the matter rest with a warning to each of you that if anything of this nature is repeated, you will be returned to the custody of your parents with the possibility of punitive legal action.

"And I will further send a note to your camp counselors that you be under their strict supervision for the remainder of your visit. Do you understand? I see that there is someone from the camp here with you. I will place the written note to the camp in her custody. I dismiss the compaint against the defendants and strongly suggest that the plaintiffs exercise more mature judgment concerning the participation of these juveniles in their research project. They would also be well advised not to rely on the testimony of juveniles on such serious legal matters. Case dismissed."

No one moved for several minutes, then the McBride Salvage company personnel walked out the door, shaking hands with each other. McBride made a point of turning and smiling at Bob.

When the Prakkes, Dr. Anderson, Bob and Karen assembled on the sidewalk, Luke was the first to speak up. "That judge had no right to do that! We told the truth, about the boat . . . and Blackbeard last night.

"Are you not going to let us be a part of the project anymore, Bob?" asked Lauren.

"Well, the judge was pretty clear about what he thought of the whole thing. I'm afraid we'll have to take his warning to heart. We can't jeopardize such an important project for the sake of entertaining you children."

"But do you believe us?" persisted Haley.

"As to what the McBride team did, of course I do. As to last night . . ."

"If you believe us about the boat attack, then you have to believe us about the ghost," demanded Lauren. We swear we saw the ghost, and that's a fact!"

Just then Karen emerged from the building. "I'd better get the kids back to camp," she said. "The magistrate gave me the dressing down of my life, but it will be mild compared to what Dave is going to say. I'll call you later, Bob."

As the kids followed Karen to the camp van, Matthew whispered, "We've got to get ourselves out of trouble if we ever want to be a part of the *Queen Anne* project again."

"How are we going to do it?" asked Lauren.

"I'm not sure," replied Matthew, "but I have an idea."

"I have a bad feeling about this," said Luke, following the others as they entered the van.

Chapter 9

Danger in the Depths

"What are we looking for?"asked Luke.

"Some evidence that the 'pirate' we saw was real," said Matthew, scanning the sand.

"If the police couldn't find anything, what chance do we have?" asked Lauren.

"It was nighttime then," replied Matthew. "Besides, I don't think they really thought we were telling the truth. And I don't believe it was a ghost."

"You looked like one last night," scoffed Lauren.

"Well, I don't believe it *now*," sniffed Matthew. "And if it was a real human being, he must have left some trace."

For hours they scoured the beach where they had seen "Blackbeard."

"Nothing," said Luke in disgust. "We might as . . . "

"What is it?" asked Haley, noticing her brother bend down to closely examine the ground at his feet. He pushed aside a clump of beach grass, reached down to pick something up, then held it aloft in triumph.

"Aha!" Luke said. "I found a clue!"

The other three gathered around him, followed by Harold and Lucy. In their midst Luke stood smiling and thoroughly enjoying his moment in the limelight. In his open hand was a strand of hemp.

"That's just an old piece of rope," said Haley, starting to turn away.

"It's not just an old rope," countered Luke. "It's a fuse."

"A what?" asked Lauren.

"A fuse, like the ones the old pirates used to light the cannon on their ships. See the burned end?"

As they bent over the object in Luke's hand, they could clearly see the singed end.

"So what does that mean?" asked Haley.

"Don't you remember the pictures of Blackbeard with those lit fuses under his hat, making the smoke curl around his head as he boarded the ships he captured?" asked Luke. "And that night . . . "

"Yeah!" exclaimed Haley. "Our 'Blackbeard' had them under his hat. I remember!"

"So a real person was pretending to be Blackbeard," pondered Luke. "But why?"

"I told you I was getting an idea," said Matthew. "Now I've got it."

"What do you mean?" questioned Lucy.

"Don't you see?" said Matthew. "Someone was hired to act like Blackbeard to frighten us . . . or make us look silly when we went to court. And it worked!"

"But how would he know we'd be there?" asked Harold.

"I don't know. But I bet the McBride Salvage Company is behind this," said Haley.

"Let's call the cops!" shouted Luke.

"Not yet," said Matthew. "They'd just say we planted this to make them believe our story. We've got to find out who was our 'Blackbeard.' "

The next day the Prakkes were once again at the camp entrance, waiting for the bus, having a heated discussion.

"You know what Dave said," warned Matthew. "One more incident and our folks will be called to come pick us up."

"Yeah, and you know how mad they'll be if they have to drive all the way down here to get us," added Luke. "To say nothing of being kicked out of camp."

"That doesn't sound like my rebel brother," said Haley.

"So why do you want to go back to see Captain Hawkins and Bob?" asked Matthew.

"Because we never got to tell them what I think the guy going into the back room was really doing," protested Haley. "I know it was one of the two guys we saw in the boat that almost hit Bob and Dr. Anderson. I've thought about it, and now I believe I know what he was doing."

"Well, I'm not going," said Matthew. "I don't want to get into any more trouble."

"Me neither," added Luke.

"I'll go with you, Haley," piped up Lauren. "I thought boys were supposed to be the big, brave types." She smiled sweetly in a way that made Luke and Matthew redden with embarrassment.

"The least you can do is distract Karen or Dave if they ask where we are," said Haley.

"Okay," said Matthew. "And we'll get Harold and Lucy to help us."

Just then the bus into Ocracoke pulled up and the two girls boarded. They sat in the back and gave a thumbs-up signal to the boys.

Soon they were standing outside of Captain Hawkins' office.

"Nobody is here," said Lauren. "I don't suppose there's any point in trying the door, after the last time." She turned the knob and the door opened.

"So much for the Captain's promise about security," said Haley. "I guess boys don't improve much when they become grown men."

The girls entered the office and went directly to the back room.

"What are you looking for?" asked Lauren.

"I'm not sure, but the only thing of value when that guy came into the office was the professors' equipment, and it was over here," replied Haley, walking over and standing in a far corner.

In the corner were a set of gauges, air hoses, empty oxygen tanks, weight belts and discarded swim fins.

"Yuck," said Lauren, wiping dust and grime from her hands as she moved the equipment around. "I don't think anyone would mess with this stuff."

"I can see that this is where the gauges are checked and the oxygen tanks are filled," said Haley, holding up a box of gaugues and shoving a full tank to the far end of the work table. "What's this?"

Lauren looked over her shoulder. "It looks like a piece of the tube that runs from a tank to the mouthpiece," she said. "And a part of a clamp."

"Yeah, but it isn't worn out like all the other pieces, it's been cut." said Haley. "Like that clamp."

"So what do you think it means?" asked Lauren, puzzled.

"That guy was back here a long time for someone just looking for something to steal," said Haley. "And now that I recall it, I remember sounds as if he were working on something."

"But what could he be working on, unless it was some of the diving equipment?"

"That's what I think," said Haley. "He was sabotaging the equipment. We've got to get in touch with Bob and Dr. Anderson quick, before something terrible happens!"

The two girls sped out of the office and ran down the street to the dock. The place where the *Arabella* was normally moored was empty, but in its place was the dinghy.

"Someone from the boat is here" said Haley. "Come on, we've got to find out who it is and get out to the boat to warn them!"

Haley and Lauren dashed from shop to shop, opening doors just long enough to see if someone from the project was inside. As they passed the diner, Lauren grabbed Haley's arm. "There's Bob!" she said.

A startled Bob turned around on his stool at the counter as the two breathless girls ran up to him.

"What's the matter?" he said. "Karen said we wouldn't be seeing you again."

"We've got to get out to the boat right away!" shouted Lauren. "We've got something important to tell the others."

"I don't know," said Bob hesitantly. "That might not be such a good idea. The magistrate was quite specific about our responsibilities regarding all of you. And Dr. Anderson has no intention of letting anything interfere with the project. I like you kids a lot, but we adults have a first priority to our work. I just came in for a quick lunch, go to the office to pick up some things, and get back out to the boat."

Speaking as rapidly as they could, and interrupting each other constantly, the two girls told Bob of their fears about the diving equipment being tampered with, which might result in tragedy.

Bob sat for a long moment, frowning. "Do you think you could quickly identify the parts that were missing from the table?" he asked Lauren. "I should go out there alone, but it would be faster if you could tell at a glance if it was on any of the tanks we took this morning." He glanced at his watch. "Dr. Anderson was going to dive this afternoon. I made him promise to wait until I got back, but if I know him, he won't."

Bob and the girls hurried to the dinghy, and in a few moments they were speeding out toward the *Arabella*.

"What's up?" said George. "That was a fast lunch. And I thought those kids were forbidden to come out here again. You're in big trouble, pal."

"Where's Dr. Anderson?" snapped Bob, leaping aboard, as the girls scampered up the ladder behind him.

"He didn't want to wait any longer," replied Andy. "So he dived off about ten minutes ago."

"Lauren, go look at those tanks back there," ordered Bob, pointing to several oxygen tanks in the stern. "See if any of them might have been the ones in the shop."

Lauren ran to the equipment and scanned each tank. All of them had old fittings and hoses. She looked at Bob and shook her head.

"We've no time to lose," said Bob. "I've got to go down there as soon as I can get fixed up. If Dr. Anderson is down there with defective equipment each moment might be a matter of life or death."

Bob's chilling words echoed in Lauren's ears as she saw him disappear down the cabin ladder to retrieve something. Without hesitation she ran to one of the tanks, slipped off her shoes, fastened on the tanks, a pair of fins and a mask. In a moment she was over the side.

Bob emerged, wearing trunks and carrying a pair of fins and a mask. "Where's Lauren?" he said.

Haley and looked around. "She was here a minute ago. She must have gone diving," said Haley, horrified.

"My god!" shouted Bob. "She's just a child! She thinks diving in the ocean is like practicing diving in a swimmiing pool. She'll drown! Help me get a tank on. Hurry!"

It took a moment for Lauren to adjust to the equipment. The oversized flippers were in constant danger of falling off, and the mask was half-filled with water. Fortunately, the tank was one of the smaller ones, and she had doubled up the straps. Because it was relatively shallow, the bottom was clear in the streams of sunlight. As she adjusted her mask, she noticed that she had been holding her breath since entering the water. She inhaled deeply through the large, ill-fitting mouthpiece, trying not to think what she would do if she couldn't breathe. If she were not underwater, she would have shouted with joy when her lungs filled with air.

She should have spit into the mask and washed it out before diving, because it kept clouding up as she frantically looked back and forth for any sign of Dr. Anderson. All she could see was the bottom rippling from the shadow of the waves overhead. All she could hear was her breathing and the bubbles that swirled around her head as she exhaled. As she floated, suspended halfway between the surface and the bottom, she saw a movement to her right.

It was Dr. Anderson! He had removed the oxygen tank on his back and was frantically fiddling with the gauge. He had let the mouthpiece fall from his mouth, and Lauren noticed that no air bubbles were coming out of it.

She swam down to him and tapped his shoulder. Initially,

Dr. Anderson did not look around at her, unaware of her presence. Lauren shoved his arm more vigorously. This time he turned around and, despite the mask, she saw the look of desperation in his eyes.

Lauren took the mouthpiece out of her mouth and offered it to the professor. Anderson wrenched it out of her hand. His motions were awkward, like those of a man in uncontrollable panic. But she quickly recovered, and with hand signals she indicated that they must share the mouthpiece as they ascended to the surface, a lifesaving technique she had learned during her YWCA diving lessons.

At first, Dr. Anderson was reluctant to surrender the mouthpiece when it was her turn, but as he regained control of his emotions, he settled into the routine of each taking two breaths, then giving up the mouthpiece. As they continued to ascend, both became aware of a shadow approaching them. It was Bob. Seeing that the breathing routine was working, he did not try to interrupt; instead, he helped guide them.

When they broke the water's surface, Bob pushed up his mask and pulled his mouthpiece from his lips.

"Dr. Anderson, are you all right?" he shouted.

Anderson nodded as he took deep breaths. "Yes . . . I'll be fine," he gasped.

Without further conversation they swam to the side of the boat and climbed aboard. Haley, Lauren, Hawkins and Bob knelt beside Anderson, who lay panting on the deck.

"My gauge malfunctioned," he finally managed to get out. Turning to Bob he said, "How could you know that was going to happen?"

"It was no accident," said Bob. "The man who broke into the Captain's office was no burglar. Apparently one of McBride's thugs altered the breathing device on the tanks. I'll bet if we check the others on board, we'll find they all have been tampered with in some manner, even the one I used. In a while it would have happened to me, too."

"What?" said Anderson.

"Ithought I recognized him," Lauren added. "Later I *knew* he was one of the two men in the boat that tried to run you down with the boat. He came into the shop to mess with the diving gear."

"I can't believe it," said Anderson. "There may be artifacts worth a lot of money aboard the *Queen Anne's Revenge*, but to attempt murder . . . "

"Maybe they didn't mean to commit murder," interjected Bob. "It could be they thought we would detect it when we checked our equipment and it would merely delay us. If so, things definitely got out of hand."

"We would have a hard time proving anything like that," said Anderson. "Especially since the testimony would once again fall upon youngsters whose reliability has been subject to question, to say the least."

Stung, Haley and Lauren lowered their eyes, staring at the deck in humiliation, which did not escape Dr. Anderson's attention.

"In any case, I owe my life to this brave young lady," he said, smiling. Impulsively, he put his muscular arms around Lauren, burying her face in his chest. Abashed at his own action, he quickly released her with an embarrased laugh. But Lauren returned his affection by hugging him around the neck and kissing his cheek.

"And what's more, I have some very exciting news," added Dr. Anderson. "Before my . . . unfortunate 'accident,' I discovered a definite debris trail which I believe to be from the *Queen Anne*. When we return to shore, I'm going to call the Institute for additional funding to rent underwater excavation equipment. Once we show them photographs of the artifacts we can bring up, I'm sure they'll give it to us. If we're lucky, we might even find enough of the wreck intact to raise her."

"Wouldn't that be something!" exclaimed Bob.

Smiling broadly, they all gave each other a round of high-fives as Hawkins started the engine.

Chapter 10

Storm

"I just gotta get back on the *Arabella* and see if they've found any gold yet," said Luke in evident frustration. "It's been almost a week, and before you know it we'll be going home!"

"I know what you mean," agreed Haley. "Besides, I want to see how the lovebirds are getting along."

"If you mean Bob and Karen, I think you can forget about that. For once your romance radar has goofed," said Lauren.

"What do you mean?" retorted Haley.

"I mean that Bob has been so immersed in his work that he's almost forgotten she exists," explained Lauren.

"Don't girls ever think about anything but that mushy love stuff?" asked Matthew.

"No," said Haley matter-of-factly. "At least, not until you boys can come up with something more interesting than looking for buried treasure and pirate ghosts."

"I've heard enough about pirate ghosts for a while," rejoined Luke.

"Glory be!" shouted Haley.

"Well, you guys go do whatever you came into town for, and we'll meet you at the diner," said Lauren.

An hour later, the girls, laden with packages, saw Matthew standing outside the diner, looking up and down the street

What's the matter?" asked Lauren, as they came up to her brother.

"I've lost Luke somewhere," replied Matthew.

"Why am I not surprised," smirked Haley. "Have you looked in the pirate section of the museum?"

"I've looked everywhere," said Matthew.

"This is the last time we take him with us anywhere," said Lauren. "He's always getting himself into trouble."

"Or us," added Haley.

"There's nowhere else to look," said Matthew. "You don't suppose he would have gone down to the boat, despite what Dave said, do you?"

The three of them looked at each other in silence. If there was anything forbidden, that is exactly where Luke would be. Without a word, they turned and walked in the direction of the boat dock.

Sure enough, the *Arabella* was at her mooring, but the Captain and the professors did not seem to be anywhere around."

"Do you see him?" asked Matthew.

"No, but I'll bet you a million dollars, he's on that boat," said Haley. "Let's go on board."

"Don't you remember what Dave, Karen, and even Bob and Dr. Anderson said?" asked Lauren, putting her hand on Haley's arm. "One more 'incident' and we're homeward bound."

"But if we don't, who knows what kind of trouble Luke will get into," observed Matthew.

That was a point of logic that none of them could argue with, and that settled the issue. They all climbed the ladder.

A quick look around revealed that Luke was not on deck, so they descended into the cabin area. It was a mess. The next few minutes were spent in tossing old clothes, charts, diving equipment, and even dirty dishes from a table onto a bunk and two deck chairs.

"I can't believe it," said a perplexed Haley, "he's not here."

"Don't be too sure," announced Lauren, lifting a sheet

that had been thrown over the table, to reveal a crouching Luke beneath..

"What're you guys doing here?" he asked, crawling out from his hiding place.

"What are *you* doing here?" countered Lauren.

"I was keeping out of the way until the boat was out to sea," said Luke. "By that time, they wouldn't turn around to take me back, after I came on deck." He smiled, without the slightest trace of guilt.

Just at that moment, the kids heard footsteps on the deck, and in another, the sound of the engine roaring to life.

"Quick! Over here," whispered Luke, pulling them over to a closet. Before they could protest, he had shoved them into it and closed it.

"Are you crazy?" hissed Lauren. "Do you want us all to get in trouble?"

"It's too late for that," said Matthew. "They're already underway."

Resigned to whatever their fate would be, the four kids stayed in the closet until the tossing of the ocean was more than they could take. Haley was the first to leave their self-imposed prison.

"I'm not sitting in here until somebody gets sick on me," she said, rising and opening the door.

"We might as well face the music," agreed Matthew.

As they ascended the steps, Lauren noticed how the boat was bouncing around in the ocean, much more than on past occasions, and the wind was strong enough that she had to grab hold of a side railing. They huddled in a group, waiting for the axe to fall.

Bob was the first to speak. "What in the world are you kids doing here?" he shouted, his face a mixture of surprise and anger.

"We wanted to sneak on board, so that we could be in on the treasure hunt," answered Matthew, bravely assuming leadership of the group. If they were going to be punished, they might as well be loyal to each other. That was a sacred Prakke characteristic.

"That is out of the question," said Dr. Anderson. "We have grown quite fond of you children, but we must abide by the wishes of the camp. We'll turn the boat around and head back to shore. Your shinanigans will cost us a full day of work."

"Perhaps we're being too hard on them, Dr. Anderson," said Bob, his voice softening. "There's a storm brewing up, and we would have to call it a day before long, in any case."

"I suppose you're right," agreed Anderson. From his tone, he appeared relieved not to reprimand the kids further.

"I'm afraid we're not heading back to shore jist yet," came Hawkins' voice from the engine hatch. "The old girl ain't respondin' like she oughta. Let me keep tinkerin' with her."

"As long as we have to wait, why don't you show us what you've found?" piped up Luke.

"Well, I suppose we might as well," groused Anderson. "Come to the back of the boat, and see what we brought up yesterday."

Bob led the group to three large metal cases wedged against the stern of the *Arabella*. He opened one and carefully lifted several clear plastic bags from it.

"Take this, for instance," he said. "This is an ordinance that, when fired, has metal wings that flared out and spun to tear sails or splinter masts. And here we have a cannon ball that exploded over the deck, showering dozens of tiny lead balls to attack the crew but not damage the ship. All this is suggestive of coming from a pirate ship, because they would not have wanted to sink the ship." Luke and Matthew stared in fascination at the lethal explosive devices.

"Don't you haveanything nonviolent to show us?" asked Lauren.

"I'll show you our greatest treasure," said Bob. Luke leaned forward, expecting to see gold doubloons. "This is a sextant, which sailors used to find out where they were by looking at the sun through it." Luke leaned back, yawning.

"Don't be so quick to scoff," advised Bob. "It is in excellent condition, one which any museum would want to have."

"Wow, you can open your own museum with all this stuff!" said Matthew.

"At least a wing of the Museum of Archives and History in Raleigh," suggested Bob with a smile.

"No gold, huh?" observed a deflated Luke.

"No gold," admitted Bob, clapping the boy on the arm. "Maybe next time."

Suddenly the bags started to slide across the deck and Dr. Anderson had to quickly replace the items into their containers and place them safely on one side of the boat. "Say, the waves are getting stronger, and the wind has picked up considerably," he said. "Bob, see if you can't hurry old Hawkins along."

Bob turned and shouted down into the engine hatch, from which came clanging sounds and muttered oaths.

"How about it, Captain?" he shouted above the increasing wind, "do you think we can get under way?"

A frightening image of a head covered with a damp handkerchief, a sweaty face streaked with oil and dirt, and an intimidating scowl emerged from the engine hatch. Bob involuntarily shrank back.

"Well, I'll tell ye, Doc," growled the old salt, "if ye'd leave me be, I might be able to fix the engine up proper." He looked up at the darkening clouds as loud rumbles of thunder attracted his attention. "But I guess she's in good enough shape to get us back to shore." He climbed up on deck and shut the hatch. He seemed startled to see the kids.

"Where'd they come from?" Hawkins asked. Without waiting for a reply, he scaled the ladder to the wheelhouse and tried to start the engine. After several failed attempts, the engine sputtered to life with an irregular rhythm. He looked over his shoulder in triumph, then pushed a lever forward.

By now rain was pouring down steadily, and the waves were tossing the *Arabella* around as if she were a toy boat. There was no use in all of them trying to crowd under the small canopy covering the wheelhouse, so everyone but Hawkins huddled together in the center of the deck. Within minutes they were all thoroughly drenched.

The *Arabella* rose and fell between the increasing swells, making way toward the shore with agonizing slowness. But as she pitched forward after cresting each wave, it seemed likely that she might capsize.

"I guess we'd better radio the Coast Guard to come get us," said Dr. Anderson, clutching Lauren and Haley firmly, while Matthew and Luke held onto the starboard railing.

"Right," agreed Bob." He staggered toward the wheelhouse, as the boat pitched wildly. The others saw him shout into Hawkins' ear, then bend over the radio.

After a few minutes, he rose, shook his head, and returned to the group. "No good. All I get is static. Looks like we'll have to try to make it in on our own."

"I wouldn't count on that," said Dr. Anderson, pointing up to the mast. As the others frantically wiped the rain from their eyes, they could clearly see that the mast had split, about three feet from the top. At any moment it might topple over the side, its weight causing the boat to capsize.

"Shouldn't we go below?" yelled Haley.

"No, we don't want to get trapped down there, in case the boat starts to sink," said Anderson. "Here, put these on as fast as you can." He opened a compartment and began handing out life preservers.

"I'll fire off a flare," volunteered Bob, reaching into a metal box at the base of the wheelhouse ladder. "I wish I could climb up the mast; the higher I am the more arc it would have."

Dr. Anderson shook his head vigorously. "In its present condition, the mast would never hold your weight. Just fire from the deck and hope for the best."

Bob loaded a a cylinder into one of the two flare guns and fired. The group groaned in disappointment as the tiny red light flickered against the dark sky, then disappeared. It would be a miracle if anyone saw it.

"It's now use, Bob," shouted Dr. Anderson. "The wind at deck level is keeping the flare from attaining sufficient height. Keep after Hawkins, to see if he can get us into shore as soon as possible."

Everyone turned to watch Bob lurch once again across the deck toward the wheelhouse. No one saw Matthew run to the signal box and extract the other flare gun and a charge.

"Hey! What's he doin'!" hollered Luke, pointing about midway up the mast.

"Stop, Matthew!" screamed Dr. Anderson, But his voice was lost in the wind. They could do nothing but watch the lone figure slowly climbing up the damaged ladder. Matthew wrapped his left arm around the tilting mast and clutch the flare gun with both hands and fired.

Instantly, the sky was illuminated by a flaming red ball that made a huge arc against the impenetrable sky. It descended in a slow path until it eventually extinguished as it entered the sea.

"Hooray!" shouted Luke, Haley and Lauren, broad grins on their faces.

At that moment a wave shook the *Arabella* violently, and to their horror they watched Matthew fall from his precarious perch!

Positioning himself just underneath, Dr. Anderson spread his massive arms out wide and enveloped the boy as he plunged toward the deck. As the two figures collapsed onto the deck, the others ran to help them up.

The professor rolled his muscular body to one side to reveal a smiling Matthew nestled in his arms. "Wow! That was really something," the boy shouted. Abruptly, the professor's face exploded into a roaring laugh. "I ought to toss you overboard for scaring us like that," he shouted, as the others helped him to his feet.

"Good work, Doctor," said Bob, coming up to the group. "Anyone within ten miles of us should be able to see that flare."

"You'll have to thank this young fellow here," said the older man, pointing to Matthew. "He's the one who risked his life to save us. If . . . *When* we get back to shore, we'll have to see he gets a hero's reward—then take him back out and keelhaul him for disobeying orders."

While Captain Hawkins continued to struggle with the

wheel, the others huddled together on the deck. The howling wind and the huge waves crashing across the deck were their only companions.

Suddenly, Haley raised her head to peer into the darkness. What was that? A light? A sound? She was about to settle back down into the comfort of the group, when she saw and heard it again.

Yes! It was definitely a light, followed by the sound of a foghorn.

"Listen up, you guys," she screamed out. "Don't you hear it? Don't you see it?"

"What?" said Luke. "I don't hear . . . Wait! I do see something." He pointed upward, where a light was playing across the clouds.

"That's just lightning," muttered Haley.

"No, it's a searchlight!" countered Luke, standing and steadying himself against Bob's arm. "Someone's shining a light and its bouncing off the clouds."

Sure enough, a round spotlight flashed back and forth on the clouds, then shot out over the water. A foghorn blasted out into the night, competing with the roar of the wind.

"The light's coming from the southeast," cried out Bob. He stood, grabbed a large flashlight beside him, and began waving it frantically from side to side.

A short time later a light played across the waves near them, eventually climbing up the stern and streaming across the deck, bathing them in its bright beam.

"Over here! Over here!" the occupants of the *Arabella* shouted, waving their arms.

"Ahoy!" boomed a voice over a megaphone. "We'll come alongside you and have crew members help you into our dinghy."

Out of the gloom the shadow of a Coast Guard cutter glided to within twenty yards of the *Arabella*. In no time several sailors lowered a dinghy into the water, and the distinct hum of its motor pierced the night. A grappling hook dug into the railing, by which the sailors pulled the dinghy close to the *Arabella*, being careful to avoid a collision.

"We'll bring all of you over in our dinghy," shouted the officer through the megaphone, "then attach a tow line to the bow of your boat to haul it into port."

"Okay, Lauren, you go first," shouted Dr. Anderson.

Lauren took a long look at the dinghy pitching wildly in the sea, then held her breath and stepped onto the rope ladder that Hawkins had lowered. She tentatively climbed down the ladder with her face buried in her arms, too frightened to cry out. She fell into the waiting arms of a sailor, then turned to wave the others on.

"Who's next?" asked Bob.

"Send Haley," said Luke, assuming an uncharacteristically protective role to his sister.

"What, so you can see where *not* to step when I fall into the ocean?" said Haley. But she climbed down, jumping into the dinghy, crossing her arms and smiling back at Luke triumphantly. In short order, Dr. Anderson and Bob made the journey; now there was only Captain Hawkins.

"Come on, old timer," yelled out one of the sailors.

Hawkins shook his head. "I ain't leavin' the old girl," he protested. "I'm stayin' aboard. I'll be all right."

"No, sir, we can't do that," shouted the officer in charge. When he saw that Hawkins did not intend to climb down he ladder, he added: "All right, but stay away from the tow line. If it breaks, it could knock you overboard."

Hawkins stood back as a gun on the cutter fired a tow line and a grappling hook onto the deck of the *Arabella*. He took the heavy tow rope and quickly fastened the hook through an iron ring on the bow. After a quick wave, he ran back to the wheelhouse and grasped the wheel.

For an hour, the cutter slowly plunged through the waves, towing the ancient ship, as Hawkins skillfully worked the wheel to keep the two vessels apart. The Prakkes and the professors watched anxiously as the old vessel ptiched violently with each wave, afraid that it would plunge beneath the water, carrying the brave old sailor with her. But they saw him smiling as he held the wheel, certain that he was singing a sea chanty.

The storm seemed to be abating as the cutter made for the dock of the Coast Guard station at Hatteras. A tug pushed against the port side of the *Arabella*, and nudged it into a mooring. When Hawkins jumped onto the dock, the others were standing together, wrapped in blankets and wait-ing for him.

Karen pushed her way through the throng, giving each other hearty congratulations and hugging each of the kids. However, when it came to Bob, he was stunned to find his outstretched arms empty. Instead, he was confronted with an icy stare and an even colder tone of voice.

"What do you mean by exposing these children to life-threatening danger?" she raged. "What kind of person are you? I thought you had a semblance of responsibility, but obviously I was mistaken!"

"But, Karen . . . " began Lauren, only to be cut off by Bob.

"No, Lauren, she's right. I was foolish from the outset to let you all be a part of this project. I'm sorry, Karen."

His apology went unacknowledged, as Karen turned abruptly around, shepherding the kids toward the camp van. Once inside, she made a quick call on her cell phone, then turned to the Prakkes. "I've just spoken to Dave. I'm sorry, but this was the last straw. He's going to call your parents and have them come down to pick you up. Until then, you are not to leave the camp."

For the first time, Karen's voice lacked that warm friendliness they had come to recognize over the past two weeks.

"What a disaster!" moaned Lauren.

"Yeah, who would have thought we'd get into such a mess," added Matthew.

"No, I mean about Bob and Karen," replied Lauren. "She won't even speak to him now."

"You've been raving about me being fixated on Blackbeard," stormed Luke. "The two of you have talked Bob and Karen since we got here. What an obsession!"

Lauren raised a silencing hand impatiently. "Quiet! I've got to think. There's got to be a way to solve this problem." The others waited in breathless anticipation, knowing it was unwise to interrupt her train of thought at such times.

"I've got it!" exclaimed Lauren. "Quick give me *all* your cash. This time it's going to take more than flowers."

"What? Again?" said Luke, incredulously. "What for?"

"For the reservation and the taxi, silly," answered Lauren.

"Huh?" chimed in Matthew.

"Another triumph, girl," said Haley, raising her hand to be smacked by a high-five from Lauren.

The boys dutifully emptied their pockets of the last of their spending money. Restricted to the camp by Dave, they had little to spend it on anyway.

As Lauren went to the camp pay phone, Luke turned to Matthew. "This love affair is costing me a fortune," he said glumly.

Six hours later, the four of them waited outside the dining hall as Fred pulled the camp jeep to a halt.

"Okay," announced Lauren, we want a full report."

"Well, the cab pulled up outside the restaurant at six o'clock," said Fred, "and Karen got out and entered the place. I could see her sitting at a table near the window. After she was seated, a waiter came up to her with a huge vase of a dozen red roses. You should have seen the look on her face!"

"Go on! Go on!" insisted Haley.

"Well, before I knew it, Bob drove up, parked his car and went into the restaurant. A waiter showed him to Karen's table. I waited for the fireworks, just like you said there might be. Karen waved him to a seat at her table, but her face looked like a stone."

"That's it?" said Luke.

"Shh!" said Haley, waving him into silence.

"I thought it would be a quick dinner, but they began talking, and eventually they were leaning toward each other.

By dessert, they were laughing and I even saw them holding hands."

"Perfect!" sighed Lauren. "Okay, here's your ten." She gave Fred a ten-dollar bill, which he pocketed and walked into the dining hall.

You're a genius, girl," said Haley, smiling at Lauren.

"Yes, I am."

The *Arabella* looked like a disaster; the railing on the port side was torn away and the mast was only a broken remnant of its former self.

"Captain, we're sorry about your boat," sighed Matthew.

"Don't you worry, lad," said the old sailor, "there's friends o' mine that can make the ole girl look brand spanking new. But it'll take a few days."

Bob and Dr. Anderson came up to the group. Bob placed a hand on the boys' shoulders. "Well, that puts a hold on our dives for a few days. But in the meantime, I have something to show you. Let's go back to the Captain's office."

In the work room, Bob put a CD into the computer. "The storm did us a great favor, really," he said. "The turbulence at that shallow depth stirred up the bottom and revealed a number of very interesting features. For instance, tell me what you see here."

""I don't see anything but an old log," said Luke.

"Not a log, my boy," replied Anderson. "That is a seventeenth century cannon, forged in Bristol, England, between 1667 and 1698. Let me show you." He keyed in a command and the image became significantly magnified. "There, you can just see where it rested on the wooden lorry, and behind that the seal of the company. It was common practice for merchant ships to arm themselves with these. They were lighter than most naval guns, but perfectly adequate to fight off most pirates."

"Those were the same kind of guns Blackbeard used on the *Queen Anne's Revenge*!" shouted Luke.

"Exactly, my boy," said Dr. Anderson. "It must have

broken off as the ship sank, and its weight ensured that it would have gone down quickly."

"That's right," confirmed Bob. "That would place the *Queen Anne* somewhere between where we were today and the Atlantic shelf."

"That would also put it between us and McBride," said Bob.

His chilling words were not lost on the group as they stared into the flickering monitor.

Chapter 11

Treasure at Last

The next week was a hectic one for the project. Unable to stand seeing the Prakkes moping around camp, Karen softened and convinced Dave to let them at least go into town, although they were not go out on the *Arabella*. But they were eager guests at Captain Hawkins' workshop. Dave had found ways to keep them busy in camp during most of the day, so it was not until late afternoon that they could catch the bus into Ocracoke. Once there, they waited on the dock until the *Arabella* docked, then joined the others to view the day's filming downloaded from the computer.

But after several days, this routine became boring. Rather than risk the others losing interest in the project, Lauren decided to boldly approach Bob to ask him for a big favor.

"Could you loan me some diving equipment so that I can teach the others how to scuba dive?" she asked.

Bob looked at her skeptically. "I know you can dive exceptionally well for your age," he said. "But are you sure you are qualified to be an instructor?"

"Why don't you watch me and make your own decision?" she suggested. "We can practice in the shallow water of the Sound, near the dock."

Consequently, Bob combed through the equipment that was stored in the back room of Hawkins' office until he had found masks, fins and tanks to accommodate the young divers, with appropriate adjustments. At first, he hid his amusement as the novices fumbled with the paraphrenalia.

When they actually entered the water and he saw the nervousness in their eyes, his heart rose up into his throat. But his doubts were soon put to rest as he witnessed Lauren's patient expertise; she was a born teacher. Matthew seemed to take easily to diving, while Haley was more hesitant.

But Luke was a different matter. Whenever he went beneath the surface he came up sputtering. "Hey, this mouthpiece is too big!" he protested after one particularly humiliating dive. Another time, his mask filled with water. "This isn't worth it!" he fumed.

"Well, if you want to dive for sunken treasure, you're gonna have to get the hang of it," said Haley airily. "Or you can just stay on the boat—if we ever get back on it."

That did it. From that time on, Haley could hardly keep him on the surface, as he struggled to master the equipment. However, the supreme moment came when Bob let them use the masks with the built-in microphones to communicate with each other.

"Xghu rct rkwin!" shouted Luke

"Turn the headset knob on your mask," said Haley. "You sound like an idiot. You know, like usual."

"This is great!" blurted out Luke in a deafening tone.

But it was Captain Hawkins that provided them the opportunity of a lifetime. Despite Dave's warning, he was sympathetic to their frustration. He sneaked them aboard the *Arabella*, and after Bob and Dr. Anderson had disappeared beneath the surface, he helped them suit up. Soon they had donned equipment and had followed the professors' trail of bubbles.

They found Anderson and Bob hovering over the cannon and photographing it. When Anderson saw them he pointed to the surface repeatedly, but the kids pretended not to see. Finally Bob shrugged his shoulders, and Anderson waved them forward. The Prakkes ran their hands over the cannon and eagerly put artifacts into baskets.

Back on the boat, Dr. Anderson sternly lectured the kids about not obeying orders, but since his rescue, he had warmed noticably, especially to Lauren, and the moment soon passed.

Two days later, the Prakkes were sitting outside Hawkins' office, impatiently waiting for the return of the *Arabella.*

"We'd better be thinking about another project," said a dispirited Matthew. "The Docs are cool, but Dave hasn't changed his mind about cancelling our part of the program."

"And I don't think we can make anything out of the film footage we have so far," added Haley.

"With our track record, I don't think Dave will want to be reminded of what we've been doing," chimed in Lauren.

"But what can we . . . hey, here comes the boat," said Lauren, pointing out to sea.

The group turned to see the *Arabella* pulling into the dock, and Bob waving enthusiastically to them.

"Do we have a surprise for you guys," Bob shouted, tossing a rope to Matthew.

"What is it?" asked Haley, caught up in the excitement of the moment.

"Let's go to the workroom and we'll show you," said Dr. Anderson. "Here, you boys take hold of the other side of this crate." Matthew and Luke grabbed the handle of the plastic crate that the professor hoisted from the boat to the dock. They struggled to keep pace with Dr. Anderson as he eagerly walked toward Sailor Hawkins' office.

In the workroom, Dr. Anderson waved the others back from the table and opened the crate. "We have here what I believe is indisputable proof that we are dealing with the *Queen Anne's Revenge*," he said.

"Or at least enough evidence to justify an extension of our grant and hire deep-sea equipment," cautioned Bob.

The Prakkes tentatively peered over the side of the crate. Expecting handfuls of golden coins to spill out onto the table, Luke's disappointment was clearly evident on his face. When Dr. Anderson carefully pulled out unrecognizable, objects, Luke frowned. "What is this junk?" he said. "Where's the treasure?"

"This *is* the treasure," corrected Dr. Anerson.

Seeing the skeptical look on the youngsters' faces, Bob hastened to add, "Legend says that Blackbeard deliberately sank the *Queen Anne's Revenge*, with a number of hands on board, in order to fool the forces seeking his capture—and to reduce the shares of his treasure. It is unlikely that he would have left gold and jewels aboard such an inaccessible location. But a manifest of items registered with the Maritime Commission that Teach listed after the sinking mentions drinking cups and cutlery with his personal crest. See here." He held up a coral-encrusted knife and spoon on which could faintly be seen a wreath with "E.T." on it.

"That's not gold," said Luke, rapidly losing interest.

"But this is exactly the kind of treasure we are seeking," said Dr. Anderson. "Remember, we want artifacts for display in museums, in order to better understand the eighteenth century. It doesn't matter if it didn't actually belong to Blackbeard. That would just be the icing on the cake."

"Whatever," said Luke, bored with the history lecture.

"Where did you get this stuff?" asked Lauren.

"This 'stuff' was among the artifacts you helped us bring to the surface," said Bob. "It may well lead us to the *Queen Anne*—if she didn't go over the Continental shelf. We'll go back tomorrow and try to verify that."

"In the meantime, I'll call the chairman of the grant committee and tell him of our find," said Dr. Anderson.

"Where're you going to keep this stuff, er, 'treasure,' " asked Hawkins.

"I suppose we'll have to leave it here," said Anderson.

"Do you think that's wise, given the trouble we've had?" posed Bob.

"What other choice have we?" replied Dr. Anderson. "I doubt we can count on the police. It seems to me they just want to be rid of the lot of us."

"Then I'm spending the night here," said Hawkins. "Any 'trespasser' will get a load o' buckshot in his tail."

"Okay," said Bob, laughing and holding up his hands. "But I think we're all being melodramatic. I'm sure there'll be no difficulty."

Walking back to the bus stop, Matthew suddenly turned to the others. "This gives our project a new life," she said.

"Why don't we come back with the video camera and take film of what the professors found?"

"Yeah, and I just thought of something," added Lauren. "If someone *does* try to break in, we can set up the camera to record it."

"You know Dave won't let us come into town after dark," said Haley. "And what would we do if someone *does* break in?

"Relax," countered Lauren. "We don't have to be here, Mr. Hawkins will be on guard. But we'll have proof that someone tried to get in, and that what we've been saying all along was the truth. All we have to do is attach a trip wire from the door to the trigger of the camera."

"What good would that do in the dark?" asked Haley.

"When the camera starts, the light will come on, like a strobe light," explained Matthew. "It will stay on long enough to show the burglar."

"Good," said Luke. "I'm tired of everyone thinking we're lying."

"Look," said Matthew. "Luke and I will stay in town and explain all of this to Captain Hawkins. Lauren, you and Haley go back to camp and get the camera, it's under my bunk. I'll call and tell Karen that we missed the bus, and we'll get a ride later."

"I thought we wanted everybody to not think we're liars," pointed out Haley.

"Well, if we walk slowly, we'll miss the bus, and we won't be lying," said Luke, with irrefutable logic.

"Okay," sighed Haley. "You're gonna grow up and be a con man." She shook her head as she watched the boys disappear down the street.

Back at camp, Lauren and Haley wolfed down a hasty supper and raced to the boys' cabin. They quickly retrieved the video camera and were walking toward the door, when Joanna, Sally and Carol appeared to block their path.

"I thought you were up to something," Joanna said.

"That's none of your business," said Lauren, attempting to walk past the intimidating trio.

"Where are you going?" asked Sally. "You know that no one is allowed to leave camp after supper without permission." She pushed Lauren back and stood in front of her, ready to back up Joanna.

"We'll talk with Karen," said Lauren.

"You've got her snowed," scoffed Joanna. "I'll just talk to Dave about this. "Some of us are sick and tired of the four of you thinking you can do anything you want and not obey the rules. It's time you were taught a lesson." With that, she laughed and abruptly shut the door.

Caught off guard, it was a moment or two before Lauren and Haley rushed to the door. Despite all their efforts, they could not open it. Turning to look at the back door, they just had time to see Carol slam it shut. In frustration, they heard the three girls standing outside the doors, jeering at their prisoners.

"Joanna is right. When she tells Dave, he'll keep us from catching the last bus to town. He'll probably ground us for the rest of our vacation. And this time Karen won't be able to help us."

"I guess we have no choice but to sit here and wait for Dave to come for us," sighed Haley, plopping onto a bunk. "We can't go out a window because it would make too much noise."

"What will the guys say?" said Lauren, joining Haley on the bunk. "They'll think we're just girls, who can't do anything right."

Suddenly they heard the doorknob of the back door rattle. Expecting to see Dave and Joanna's smirking faces, they were surprised to see Lucy and Harold smiling triumphantly.

"Where did you guys come from?" asked Lauren in disbelief. "What happened to Joanna and her toadies?"

"Come see for yourself," said Lucy, stepping aside and waving her hand toward the lawn leading to the woods.

Following them outside, Haley and Lauren saw a canvas tarp, under which several bodies struggled. Stout ropes fastened the tarp to two nearby trees, and the corners were staked into the ground.

"What's this?" asked a puzzled Haley.

"We thought the 'Dragon Lady' was up to something when she left after you guys ran out of the dining hall, so we followed her," said Arnold. "And when we saw her lock the door, we set up an ambush and threw the tarp on top of them." He preened and strutted like a peacock.

"They were so startled that they couldn't get out from under the tarp before we had it secured," added Lucy.

"What are you going to do with them?" asked Lauren. "You can't keep them under there forever."

"We'll let them out after you've gone," said Lucy. "Until then, Harold brought his guitar, and several of us will sing songs for an hour or so. Very loudly."

"You're really swell friends," said Lauren, softly punching Lucy's arm.

"Go on with ya," said Harold, waving them away. "Or else Dave might see you. After we let the 'Dragon Lady' and her newts out, we can't cover for you, so you'd better hurry."

With a final wave, the girls ran for the front gate to catch the last bus for town.

Chapter 12

Catching the Crooks

"Okay, so where do we put the camera?" asked Haley.

"Over here," said Lauren, pointing to the far corner of the workroom, near the ceiling. "I'll have to fix up a frame to hold it."

"Won't the burglar just reach up there and yank it down?" asked Haley.

"I bet that he'll be so surprised that he'll run away. Besides, I'm gonna tape it to the rafters so that it will be too much trouble for him to mess with."

Lauren put a stepladder under a rafter and secured the camera to it, as Haley dutifully handed her tools on demand. Just as she was descending the ladder, Captain Hawkins walked in, carrying an ancient shotgun.

"What are you going to do with that blunderbuss," asked Lauren. "Hunt for elephants?"

"Don't you worry, I can deal with any intruders with this baby," said Hawkins, patting the barrel.

"Yeah, maybe by scaring them to death," snorted Haley.

Hawkins looked up at the camera. "So you think you'll get a shot of any burglar yourself with that, do ye?" he asked. "I don't know nuthin' about them things, so who's goin' to look after it?"

"We took a vote and decided not to go back to camp," said Lauren. "Our friends are going to cover for us while we wait here and see what happens."

"What's that big shot back at camp goin' to say about that?" asked Hawkins, fixing them with a skeptical eye.

"I don't fancy gettin' myself in trouble over ye." But the girls could see a glint in his eye, and the trace of a smile in the corners of his mouth.

"Well, if you don't see us, you can't get in trouble over us, can you?" asked Haley impishly.

"No, I reckon not," said the old sailor, nodding. "But I wouldn't say anythin' to the perfessers. They may not take kindly to the idea."

Luke looked as if he were going to explode, curled up in the back of the camp truck as it made its weekly trip to get supplies at Bath. Matthew, however, lay stoically silent against a crate.

"I think this is a nutty idea," muttered Luke. "Why didn't Captain Hawkins take us to see him when we went on the tour here?"

"Because he didn't want any competition for his reputation as an authority on Blackbeard," said Matthew. "Or it might have slipped his mind." He reached into his pocket for the torn brochure that he had found in Hawkins' back room. At first he ignored it until, on closer inspection he recognized a familiar face.

"Well, how do you know this guy's still doin' his show?" continued the ever-skeptical Luke. "That brochure looks old. And how do you know it's the same guy?"

"It's the only clue we've got," responded Matthew, so we'll just have to hope for the best."

An hour later the truck came to a stop. The two boys carefully peeked out from the canvas tarpaulin to watch Fred go into a small grocery store. Then they crawled out over the tailgate.

"Okay, let's get to work," said Matthew matter-of-factly. "There's no telling when Fred will be back. We'll walk down this way. The brochure says the theatre is on Roanoke Street.

They walked slowly down the street, weaving in and out of groups of tourists, pausing at old buildings, only to walk on in frustration. Finally Luke grabbed Matthew's arm and pointed toward a stairway descending from the street and into an alleyway. "Look, there it is!"

Matthew looked in the direction his cousin was pointing, but saw nothing, other than an old poster peeling off of a brick wall.

"What?" said Matthew. "I don't see anything but that old poster."

"It *is* the poster!" said Luke excitedly. "Come on!"

Luke pulled a puzzled Matthew over to the steps and ran rapidly down the steps. At the bottom, they stood before a faded and torn poster. Staring down at them was the picture of an actor, James Todd, the embodiment of the pirate Blackbeard!

"Okay, you win," said Matthew. "Let's see if we can get in. He pressed against the door, but it was locked. About to turn away, he was startled to see Luke banging furiously on the door. "Hey, what are you doing?"

Luke didn't answer, but continued to pound on the door. Eventually it was opened by a wizened old man, only a little taller than the boys, with a bald head festooned with prominent veins.

"The theatre don't open till seven-thirty," he said in a surly tone.

"We want to see Mr. Todd," said Matthew, putting his foot in the doorway to prevent the old man from closing it.

"He don't see nobody," said the truculent doorman. He stepped on Matthew's foot to make him move it.

"Just tell him we know all about the night out on the dunes," Matthew shouted through the closed door.

"Guess that was a bummer," sighed Luke.

"Let's wait a minute," said Matthew. "I think he'll want to talk to us."

Moments passed without any noise from the other side of the door. After a few more moments, they looked at each other, and Matthew shrugged his shoulders in defeat. Just as they were turning to ascend the steps, they heard the door opening. They turned to see the old man impatiently waving them towards him.

"Todd says he'll talk to you," snapped the old man. "But hurry up. I ain't got all day to fool with you kids."

The doorman ushered the boys down a dark hallway that smelled dank. He stopped outside a door and knocked.

"Come in," said a gruff voice. The old man opened the door, and turned to go back down the hallway.

Matthew and Luke peered into the room to see a large, burly man in eighteenth century clothing looking into a stage mirror. He was braiding red ribbons into the wild strands of a bushy black beard.

He turned around. "Well, what do you want?" he said. "I don't give out autographs until after the show."

Before them stood the Blackbeard of the dunes!

"We're not interested in the show," said Matthew, finding his voice. "Not *this* show, anyway."

The actor looked at them sharply. "What do you mean? And what was that about 'the night at the dunes?' "

"We saw your 'performance' last Thursday night near the YMCA camp at Ocracoke," said Luke. "As a matter of fact, we know you put it on, just for our benefit."

"I don't know what you're talking about. Now get out of here before I call old Jenkins to have you thrown out." He sounded menacing, but the boys could detect an undertone of nervousness in his voice.

"Oh, you had us believing you were Blackbeard's ghost, all right," countered Matthew. "At first, I didn't recognize you as the man at 'Blackbeard's Castle' until I saw the brochure about your performance here, too. Then I knew it was you on the dunes. And you must know there was something not right about it, or else you wouldn't be talking to us."

"That does it!" shouted Todd, abruptly standing to tower over the boys, who inadvertently shrank back. "I was never out at any Y camp. Why would I do a fool thing like that? I was here, putting on my show, as usual."

"We say you were out there, and we know why," said Matthew. "And here's the proof." He held out the length of rope that Luke found in the sand. "You put them under your hat and light them during your act. Like Blackbeard did."

Todd looked at the piece of rope. "You can't prove that is one of the props of my act."

"We'll turn it over to the police," added Luke. "They can look for stands of hair from a beard. And they can do DNA tests to see if those hairs came from *your* hair."

Todd stared at them for a few moments, during which the boys prepared to run out the door if he tried to grab the rope from Matthew's hand. But instead of advancing toward them, he seemed to wilt before their eyes. He slumped into a chair and let his chin sink onto his chest.

"Okay, you're right," said softly. "I was out at the camp last week. I tried to convince myself that it was a harmless way to promote my act, which is about to be cancelled by the theater. But I knew there was more to it."

"Did McBride hire you?" asked Matthew.

Todd nodded. "He said he wanted to drum up interest in his salvage operation, and a newspaper story about frightened kids would be just the thing. But when nothing came out in the paper or on TV, I knew he had something else in mind, probably illegal. So instead of trying to make a buck out of it for my show, I just kept my mouth shut." He looked up at the boys. "You're not going to go to the cops, are you? I barely make a living playing Blackbeard to small groups of tourists; it's all I can do. I'm not the greatest actor in the world."

Luke and Matthew looked at each other, then back at the actor. "Are you willing to tell this story to the police, if we say that we don't think you were involved in a crime?"

Todd nodded, a look of resignation and relief in his eyes. The boys walked out the door. Matthew paused. "I wouldn't worry about the police, if you keep your word," he said. "And as to your not being a good actor, all I can say is, that you sure scared the bezeesus out of us that night."

A faint smile played across the actor's features as he watched the boys walk rapidly down the hallway.

"That was about the best luck we've had so far," said Luke. "I never thought he'd admit what he did. I guess that will show the cops that we weren't lying."

"Yeah," agreed Matthew. "And if we were right about Blackbeard's ghost, then maybe they'll think we were right about McBride's crew threatening Bob and Dr. Anderson with their boat and tampering with the diving gear. But right now, we'd better get back to the truck, or else we're in big trouble."

The boys raced back to the store, only to see the truck pulling away from the curb.

"Hurry!" shouted Matthew, and raced for the disappearing vehicle, with Luke right behind. Matthew leaned forward and just grabbed the tailgate. He held on in desperation, his feet dragging behind him. Gritting his teeth, he pulled himself up and over the tailgate. He immediately turned around to grasp Luke's wrist just as his cousin's hand slipped from the tailgate. Matthew fell onto his back, pulling with all of his strength, finally feeling Luke's weight upon him.

The boys sat up, breathing heavily and staring at each other. Evenually Luke gasped out, "Don't . . . you think it would . . . have been easier . . . to just take the bus?"

Matthew looked at him for a moment, then burst into uncontrolled laughter.

The sunlight coming from the small window in the back room faded slowly, and Haley and Lauren found themselves in darkness.

"You're sure this is going to work?" asked Haley.

"It'd better, or else we're in big trouble," replied Lauren.

"Yeah, I think McBride can be pretty rough, if he wants to be," mused Haley.

"I was thinking more of Dave," said Lauren.

At that moment, they heard a noise in the outer office, which caused each to hold her breath. To their great relief they saw Hawkins standing in the doorway.

"Just want to let you know that I'm going to check out back. Thought I heard a noise."

"Gee willicurs, Captain, you scared us out of our wits," said Haley, exhaling loudly.

Hawkins laughed, then turned to walk out the front door of the office. "You don't need to worry about anything as long as the old Captain's here," he said over his shoulder.

"Maybe we should have asked the police to be here with us," said Haley.

"What, and have them laugh and take us back to camp?" said Lauren dismissively.

"Well, at least Bob and Dr. Anderson," replied Haley. "Somehow, this doesn't seem like a good idea now."

"Because it's gotten dark?"

"Yeah."

Another hour crept by, although it seemed much longer, and the two of them stretched their aching muscles.

"I thought the whole idea of the hidden camera was so we wouldn't have to be here," whispered Haley.

"I'm not taking any chances on the camera not working again," explained Lauren. "And if we do get lucky and film someone from McBride Salvage stealing artifacts, we'll need to be able to testify as to exactly what the camera recorded."

"This could be very dangerous," said Haley.

"We learned from the other break-in that if we're quiet and keep our eyes open, nothing will happen to us. It will be like . . . "

Lauren's explanation was cut short by the sound of the lock of the front door being forced open. A shadow blocked out most of the moonlight streaming in through the door. From the shape of the figure, the girls could tell that this time it was not the Captain.

Lauren clasped Haley's forearm and looked up to the camera, heartened to see the red "record" button gleaming in the darkness. She only hoped that Matthew's infrared lens would be adequate to capture images in the darkness.

The door closed and the girls heard stealthy footsteps advancing into the back room. The noises emanating from the darkness indicated that the intruder was putting artifacts from the shelves into a container. Then the footsteps approached the safe, where the most important items lay.

The flashlight beam fell upon the combination lock. A gloved hand turned the lock back and forth, the tumblers clicking loudly. The door to the safe opened and the girls heard the sound of objects being placed into a bag.

At that moment the strobe light flashed.

"What in the . . . " said a voice, and the beam of the flashlight swung around to play across the shelving near the ceiling. It stopped when it landed on the camera.

Instead of running, the figure grabbed a chair and stood on it, pulling the camera from its perch. Footsteps strode rapidly to the light switch on the wall, and the room was immediately bathed in light from the bulb on the ceiling.

A gasp of surprise escaped Haley's lips. The man holding the camera was the same man who had been at the wheel of the boat that almost ran down Bob and Dr. Anderson, and almost certainly the same man who had broken into the office the first time. He looked over at the place where the girls were croutched behind the filing cabinet.

"Come out of there, you two," he shouted gruffly.

Tentatively, the girls rose from their hiding place and stood in the harsh glare of the naked light bulb.

"You can't get away with it this time," said Lauren, trying to make her voice sound calm. "Even if you destroy the camera, we'll be able to testify about what you did here."

"You're making it tough on yourselves," said the man

"You won't do anything to us," said Haley defiantly. "There's a man outside who has heard everything, and is probably calling the police right now."

"Was he wearing a hat like this?" came an ominous voice from the door.

The girls turned to see McBride standing in the doorway, holding the Captain's battered cap. There was an ugly spot of blood near the brim. A chill ran through them. "What are you going to do with us?" asked Haley.

"Don't be melodramatic," said McBride. "I'm not going to tie cinder blocks to your ankles and dump you into the Sound," said McBride, smiling. "I don't have to. I've spent too much time in discrediting you in the eyes of the law.

Although I must admit it, dumping you in the ocean has its appeal. You've caused me a great deal of trouble."

"When you display these artifacts, everyone will know that you stole them," said Lauren, "and you'll be arrested."

"But no one will see these relics, at least not publicly," laughed McBride. "I intend to sell them to private collectors, who will be content just to have them. Those sales should make me enough money to raise the *Queen Anne's Revenge*, and *that* will be where I will get rich."

"Bob and Dr. Anderson will see to it that you won't get away with it," shouted Haley, her anger giving her courage. "And we'll tell everyone what you've done."

"It will be amusing to see their reputations ruined by making irresponsible charges based on the testimony of children exposed as pathological liars."

Haley wasn't sure what "pathological" meant, but it didn't sound good. Without the film evidence it would be another frustrating case of the authorities not believing them. And this time, it would be Bob and Dr. Anderson being in trouble. She knew what slander and libel were, and making false charges against someone. At the very least, they would be the laughing stock of their professions, and probably lose their jobs. And it would be partly her fault.

Haley nudged Lauren's arm with her elbow and nodded toward the camera in the first intruder's hands. Lauren saw that the red light was still on. In his haste, the man had not thought to turn it off. So everything that had been said was being recorded. They had to get that camera.

Lauren ran to the desk, picked up a heavy metal ruler and ran to the window. With a wide sweep of her arm, she broke the glass, shattering it.

As McBride ran at Lauren, Haley rushed at the thug holding the camera. She wrenched it out of his hands and ran toward the door. Heavy footsteps thudded behind her as she fled out into the moonlight. Another figure run from a panel truck parked on the street. Without thinking, Haley darted into an alley. She bumped into a garbage can, stumbling backward as it rolled over and over, clanging its way down the alley. In panic she turned and ran into the darkness, until she came up against a wooden fence towering above her.

Turning around, Haley saw two figures advancing down the alley, their shadowy forms silhouetted by a streetlamp. Clutching the camera tightly, she shrank back against the fence as the figures advanced toward her.

Two shadows suddenly appeared behind those menacing Haley.

"Oh no you don't!" came the voice of Captain Hawkins.

In the dim light she saw him shove the barrel of his shotgun into the stomach of one of the thugs, then bring it down upon his back. The man staggered backward, then collapsed.

But Haley had no time to linger over that scene, for the other man was now looming over her. He reached out to pull the camera from her, but she held on stubbornly. When he raised his hand to strike her, she shut her eyes, waiting for the blow.

From out of nowhere a hand grabbed the man's arm and pulled it behind his back. The two figures struggled in the darkness of the alley, each breathing heavily. At first, the thug seemed to be gaining the advantage over Haley's mysterious rescuer, but gradually he bent under the grip of his antagonist. With a final blow, the thug fell on the ground and lay still.

Hardly daring to open her eyes, Haley tentatively looked up to see Bob's smiling face staring down at her. She gasped with delight and rushed to him, throwing her arms around his waist.

"You don't have to worry about that jerk anymore. He can't hurt you now," said Bob, bending down to look into her eyes.

In the office, Lauren felt herself being jerked around by McBride, who clapped a hand over her mouth to prevent her from screaming out the open window.

"Maybe it *would* be better to get rid of you kids, once and for all," he growled, holding her in a vice-like grip.

"I don't think so," said a deep voice. McBride was pivoted around and shoved against the wall. As he stood up, Dr. Anderson decked him with a well-placed punch to the jaw. McBride rose up on one elbow, then sank back to the floor, moaning.

Dr. Anderson enfolded Lauren in his huge, hairy arms. "I'm not about to let anything happen to *my* rescuer—and my very special little friend," he said, smiling broadly.

Soon, McBride and his two accomplices were in handcuffs. The small office space was filled with the three crooks, Haley, Lauren, Bob, Dr. Anderson, Karen, Hawkins, Fred, the county sheriff and a deputy.

"How did you know we were here?" Lauren asked Bob.

"Karen called and said she'd had second thoughts about covering for you," answered Bob. "It seems you've managed to impress her with your impulsiveness—and your courage. Dr. Anderson and I guessed what you had in mind, although it didn't take a rocket scientist to figure it out, once Karen discovered that the camera was missing among your things.

"And when we found the Captain lying in the alley, I knew we had to act fast. Fortunately, Karen had called the police from the camp."

Bob's narrative was interrupted by Matthew and Luke bursting into the room, accompanied by another police officer and Fred.

"Looks like ye missed all the excitement," said Hawkins, tenderly, touching the bandage on his forehead.

Luke was flabbergasted as Haley gave him a big hug, but he disentangled himself from her embrace and stepped away. "Cut it out, will ya?" he said. "You're okay."

After explaining everything to the Sheriff, Matthew asked, "Mr. Todd is not gonna be prosecuted, is he?"

The sheriff shook his head. "No, we're convinced he was not part of McBride's scheme. He's just an actor who was hired for a role, and he played it up to the hilt."

"But how did he know when we'd be out at the dunes?"wondered Luke.

"I think Fred can answer that, right Fred?" said Bob.

"Yes, sir," mumbled Fred, stepping forward. "Mr. McBride had approached me about pulling the stunt to get publicity for his salvage. When I overheard Luke asking Matthew to go with him to take a shower after curfew, I called Mr. Todd to go out on the dunes. I signaled to him that the kids were coming. I swear I had no idea there was anything more to it. At first I thought it was neat, with all the excitement caused when the kids came tearing back into camp, and went along with the gag. But when I saw how scared they were, I began to worry that I would get fired, so I didn't say anything to anyone."

"I believe you," said Dr. Anderson. "And I've talked with the sheriff to make a recommendation to the District Attorney that you be given a severe reprimand and nothing more when this case comes to trial."

"What charges will be filed against Mr. McBride?" asked Lauren.

"Well, for starters, assault, reckless endangerment, fraud, breaking and entering, burglary," answered the sheriff. "I think there'll be enough trouble to keep Mr. McBride busy for quite some time."

"And maybe this will be a good lesson to those tempted to steal and illegally sell historic artifacts," added Anderson.

"How are you going to explain all of this in court?" asked Haley.

"That's the easy part," said Karen. "I'm wondering how we're going to explain it to your parents!"

The resulting video presentation was one of the best end-of-camp programs in the history of Camp Ocracoke. To no one's surprise, Luke had a starring role, although he graciously gave significant supporting roles to Lucy and Harold—and even the girls. At the end of the program, Dave sheepishly praised the quality of the film. He seemed embarrassed that he had ever argued against the project, and led the campers in a standing ovation for the Prakkes.

But the real treat for the Prakkes came after the program, speeches and the picnic. Bob, Karen and Dr. Anderson came over to where the kids were standing and introduced themselves to their parents. Then, after several minutes of pleasant conversation, Bob turned to the kids and said, "Well, we have spoken to your folks, and we have a special treat in store for you."

"What?" asked Matthew.

"You're all invited on a special dive this afternoon. How does that sound?"

"Hooray!" the four kids shouted in unison.

By 1:00 the Prakke kids, Bob, Karen, Dr. Anderson and the Captain were aboard the *Arabella*, bobbing in the Sound.

Bob turned to the kids as they donned diving gear. "Now, you're still relatively new at this, so stay close to me or Dr. Anderson. Fortunately, we won't be down very deep."

"Just watch me," said Lauren. "I'll show you what you should do."

One by one they plopped into the water. Dr. Anderson had provided them with the masks fitted with microphones, so they could communicate with each other. Bob and Dr. Anderson waited patiently as the kids looked around in awe at the beauty of the underwater world. At last, Dr. Anderson waved them forward, and they swam leisurely through the schools of fish that surrounded them, the light rippling over their bodies and the ocean floor.

"Say, where's he taking us?" asked Matthew, noting that the professors seemed to have a definite purpose in mind.

"I don't know," replied Haley excitedly, "but I have an idea."

Gradually a shape began to form in the distance; in a few moments the group began to swim downward, following the slope of the ocean floor. As the divers approached the vague form, they could see that it was the rotting remains of an eighteenth century ship. Bob proudly posed beside the faded plaque on the bow. *Queen Anne's Revenge*.

They had done it!

"Hallelujah!" exuded Luke, swimming forward to glide

over the remnants of where the wheel had stood, and the yawning interior, once covered by the deck that had rotted away over two centuries ago.

"We were lucky," said Dr. Anderson, "another hundred feet and she would have gone over the Continental shelf."

"Hold on, Luke," cautioned Bob, placing a restraining hand on the boy's shoulder. "This is a very fragile site, and quite dangerous."

"Where's the treasure?" asked Luke.

"It will take a long time to carefully search the interior of the ship," said Dr. Anderson. "For the time being, we'll have to be content to retrieve items from the debris field surrounding the vessel."

"What we wanted for now was to give you the opportunity to see the ship as its been, undisturbed for over two hundred years. Maybe someday we'll be able to ask you to join us in actually raising it. And no going inside for now."

"Okay," Luke said, in a decidedly disappointed tone.

"Don't be a spoil sport," criticized Lauren. "This is the chance of a lifetime. Come on!"

For the next thirty minutes, the kids were carefully led around the exterior of the ship by Dr. Anderson and Bob, who pointed out various features. But eventually the professors had to order them to the surface. Just before they ascended, Dr. Anderson reached down among the objects half-buried in the sand, shook it and offered it to Luke.

Back aboard the *Arabella,* Luke turned the object over and over in his hands. It was a silver drinking cup, with an elaborate handle. "Wow! Is it valuable?" he asked.

"Only historically," answered Bob. "We can't let you keep it, but we thought you'd like to have actually handled something that Blackbeard used. When I saw it, I immediately thought of you."

"It makes me feel like I was a pirate on his ship!" said Luke, brandishing the mug as if he were about to take a drink.

"Ahoy, Matey!" shouted Dr. Anderson, amid raucous laughter.

Chapter 13

The Real Treasure

The newspapers were filled with the discovery of the *Queen Anne's Revenge*, and the dramatic circumstances of the retrieval of its artifacts. As Bob and Dr. Anderson had hoped, the publicity led to an expanded project that would perhaps one day raise the old ship.

Meanwhile, The Department of Archives and History in Raleigh hosted a display of the artifacts. Dr. Anderson and Bob arranged for the Prakkes to be prominent guests at the festivities surrounding the gala opening of the display. The kids in turn made sure that Captain Hawkins, Harold and Lucy received invitations to join them in the distinguished guests section with them. They also sent an invitation to Joanna Livingston, but she did not attend.

The event included speeches from state dignitaries and the staff of the Department, and an endless photo session by reporters and photographers, and tables groaning with all sorts of delicious refreshments. And as a special request of the kids, James Todd was a featured guest, bedecked in his most flamboyant Blackbeard costume, complete with smok-ing ropes under his hat and ribbons in his flowing black beard, and sporting an appropriately intimidating sneer.

It was all so overwhelming that even the irrepressible Luke was subdued. It wasn't until they were standing with their parents and grandparents, and friends at the table of goodies that the kids felt comfortable enough to relax.

"Well, Captain, I see you have really spruced yourself

up," said Bob, clapping his hand on the sailor's arm. "I hardly recognized you." Haley scrunched up her mouth skeptically. True, the old salt had on a wide red tie with yellow flowers and a blue suit jacket, but he still wore his battered cap and the jacket had weathered patches on the elbows. But you would have thought from his smiling face, that he was dressed in white tie and tails.

"Well, sir, I'll tell ye, I thought I owed it to my young shipmates here, to dress up in me finery. After all the publicity in the newspapers, my tour and charter business is goin' good. Gave the *Arabella* a complete overhaul, and the ole gal looks real pretty."

"Here is another special guest," said Dr. Anderson, spreading his arms. Todd gave a bear hug to each member of the group

"Arrgh, Mateys, you're looking at the hottest show on the Outer Banks." he said. "I'm even going to give performances up and down the Atlantic coast this fall. There was a time that I thought I might be going to jail, but instead I'm a celebrity." He gave a wink to one and all. "That's a much better way to be wanted, I'll tell ye." Everyone's laughter was interrupted by the raucous squeal of the sound systerm.

"Ladies and gentlemen," announced the Director of the Archives and History Department, who was serving as Master of Ceremonies. "May I have your attention, please. Let me direct you to the center of the room, where a short presentation will be made.

"The Smithsonian Institution in Washington has been working with us in the display of the *Queen Anne's Revenge* artifacts, and has graciously created a special award for some very special friends of ours. Without the contribution of the Prakke children, this display may well not have been possible. In their honor, it is our privilege to present each of them with a medallion commemorating this occasion."

A staff member strode forward to the group surrounding the Prakkes. With great dignity he presented each with an open box in which rested a circular bronze medal, to which was attached a red, white and blue ribbon. Using a portable microphone, he began speaking.. "The inscription reads: 'In grateful appreciation for participation in the *Queen Anne's Revenge* Restoration Commission Project. Department of Archives and History, Raleigh, North Carolina.' "

Applause echoed throughout the room as the Prakke kids accepted the boxes, their faces blushing. A photographer asked them to hold up their medals as he snapped a series of pictures.

Bob and Karen joined the group as everyone was admiring the kids' medals.

"I've got a medal of my own to show off," said Karen. She stretched forth her left hand to reveal a sparkling diamond engagement ring on her third finger.

"Congratulations!" said Dr. Anderson, hugging her. "Or is it 'best wishes to the bride'?"

"Either one will be just fine," Karen said, kissing the professor on the cheek. Then everyone proceeded to shake Bob's hand. Lauren and Haley gave each other a very self-satisfied nod and knowing smile.

To everyone's surprise Luke abruptly walked past the display case of the gold coins that he had recovered, to another display case. Surrounded by his sister and cousins, parents, grandparents and friends, he pointed to an object on display. It was the drinking vessel that Bob had given him on their dive to the *Queen Anne*. At its base was a small sign that read: "Retrieved by Luke Prakke." Several other objects displayed similar notation identifying each of the Prakkes as the retriever of the object.

"All summer I've been talking about getting rich by finding pirate gold and treasure," Luke said, beaming a broad smile. "But listening to the professors talk about history and all, now I know that this is the *real* treasure."

Bibliography

Stick, David. *The Outer Banks of North Carolina, 1584-1958*. University of North Carolina Press: Chapel Hill, 1958.

Roberts, Nancy. *Blackbeard and Other Pirates of the Atlantic Coast*. John F. Blair: Winston-Salem, N.C., 1993.

Wheedbee, Charles Harry. *Blackbeard's Cup and Stories of the Outer Banks*. John F. Blair: Winston-Salem, N.C., 1989.

. *Outer Banks Tales to Remember*. John F. Blair: Winston-Salem, N.C., 1985.